tHE JUNIOR NOVEL

Adapted by Peter Lerangis

Screenplay by Christopher Nolan and David S. Goyer
Story by David S. Goyer

Batman Created by Bob Kane

SCHOLASTIC INC.

New York   Toronto   London   Auckland   Sydney
Mexico City   New Delhi   Hong Kong   Buenos Aires

ISBN 0-439-72509-7

Photos courtesy of Warner Bros.
Designed by Rick DeMonico

12 11 10 9 8 7 6 5 4 3 2 1   5 6 7 8 9/0

Printed in the U.S.A.
First printing, June 2005

PROLOGUE

At the center of the city stood a tower. It rose as if thrust up from the bedrock itself, a beacon of steel and glass that pulsed with the lifeblood of Gotham. Through its chambers streamed the people of the city, sustained by the constant thrum of pipe and cable. Flesh, fuel, water, power – they flowed all day over river and cement, track and road, tunnel and viaduct, all vessels leading inevitably to and from the center.

For generations, Wayne Tower had been the heart of Gotham.

But a healthy heart cannot exist without a soul. Weaken one, and the other follows. A soul decays. A heart breaks.

When it happens, the descent is swift. A choice must be made.

Give in to the darkness.

Or reach into its core, into the chittering shrieks and the shudder of shadows.

Where one wrong move can lead to death.

And where salvation may be found on the wings of a bat.

He belonged here. Somehow, it seemed right that he'd ended up in this miserable prison, half a world away from Gotham City. It was a place where rats outnumbered humans and it was hard to tell the difference. A fitting tribute to a life of comfort and wealth that had collapsed of its own weakness.

Bruce Wayne shuffled forward in the food line. His twenty-eight years weighed heavily on him, as if each year had been a lifetime. He kept to himself, trusting nothing. Trust was a poison. It lifted you on lies and dropped you without warning. In the flick of a finger, a flash of light, a curling wisp of gun smoke, it shattered your soul.

As he took his gruel and turned from the table, his plate was swiped away by a hulk of muscle and evil intention whose name he did not know.

"You are in hell, little man . . ." The prisoner did not speak English well, but his fist communicated loud and clear with Bruce's jaw. ". . . and I am the devil."

Bruce sprawled to the ground but sprang back upward, ignoring the pain. "You're not the devil," he replied, staring now at not one but seven enormous prisoners. "You're practice."

They jumped fast. Two of them took Bruce by the arms. He lashed upward with his legs, knocking out two of the attackers instantly.

CCRRRRACK!

At the sound of the gunshot, all prisoners hit the deck. Released, Bruce sank to the muddy ground and heard the word that had become all too familiar: "Solitary!"

As a prison guard yanked him upward, Bruce shook free. "Why?" he asked.

"For protection," the guard replied.

"I don't need protection," Bruce protested.

The guard pointed to the inert prisoners at Bruce's feet. "Protection for *them*."

The guard threw Bruce onto the cell floor and slammed the door shut. The room fell into a darkness relieved only by a sliver of hallway light through the door's slatted window.

"I often wonder at the riches to be found in dark places. . . ."

Bruce spun around at the unexpected voice. He saw the silhouette of a man in the corner.

"These men have mistaken you for a criminal, Mr. Wayne." The man's voice, which hinted of a European education, was as much a surprise as the very fact that he was here. He rose, unfolding a tall, powerfully built frame. His tailored suit and silk tie were as out of place as a grilled steak on the gruel table. "My name is Ducard, but I speak for Rā's al Ghūl. Have you heard the name?"

Bruce nodded. Perhaps the question was meant

to be polite, but it assumed that he knew nothing of the criminal world. Bruce had lost that innocence long ago. "I've heard the legends – master warrior, international mercenary, feared by all the under-world. Some even swear he's immortal."

"Rā's al Ghūl uses theatricality and deception as powerful weapons," Ducard said. "You have not escaped his notice. A man like you is here by choice . . . or because he is truly lost."

Lost? The words cut to the core of Bruce's soul.

"Rā's al Ghūl and his League of Shadows offer a path to those who are capable of upholding our code," Ducard continued.

"Code?" Bruce said. "Aren't you criminals?"

"A criminal is simply a man who someone else thinks should be put in jail." Ducard gestured out-ward, toward the prison guards. "This world is run by tyrants and corrupt bureaucrats. Our code respects only the natural order of things. We're not bound by their hypocrisy. Are you?"

With a cock of his head, Ducard walked to the door and knocked sharply. Instantly a guard pulled it open. "There is a rare flower," Ducard said, pausing in the doorway, "a blue, double-bloomed poppy that grows on the eastern slope. Tomorrow you will be released. Pick one of the flowers. If you can carry it to the top of the mountain, you may find what you are looking for."

"And what am I looking for?" Bruce asked.

An indefinable expression – concern? pity? – flickered across Ducard's face.

"Purpose," he said.

2

Who was he?

Somehow Ducard had managed to shorten his sentence — how did he do it? How could a total stranger know so much about him?

Bruce sank onto the hard wooden bench. He was tired but dreaded sleep. He hated solitary confinement. Not because of the deprivation or the darkness but because of himself. His own mind. Without the fighting, without the movement and the grit of prison life, all he was left with were time, dreams, and memory.

Memory always brought him to the place he feared most.

Slowly the darkness closed around him like a fist, and he finally surrendered.

Once again, it is the day. The day it all began.

Bruce is eight years old, in a field of flowers. Their petals tickle his feet as he runs, laughing, chasing a girl's laughter.

The girl's hair flashes gold as she disappears around the corner of the house. It is a fortress of imported stone and hand-cut glass — known to the rest of the world through photographs and awed whispers as Wayne Manor. To Bruce, however, it is just home.

He races around the corner. Seeing the open greenhouse door, he smiles. Rachel knows these grounds well. She lives on the Wayne estate with her mother, Mrs. Dawes, the housekeeper. Rachel is very smart — but not smart enough to fool Bruce.

The greenhouse air is warm and thick as he steps inside. He surveys the long tables of flowers, their tendrils and blossoms spilling over the edges. "Rachel?" he calls out.

A hand covers his mouth, and he is dragged

under the table, sputtering. "I'm kidnapping you," Rachel says. "They'll pay a lot for precious Brucie."

Outside, Mrs. Dawes calls their names. They fall silent — but as Mrs. Dawes's footsteps retreat, Bruce bolts. Out the door . . . around the house . . . to the old stone well. It hasn't been used in years. A few feet below the lip of the well is a platform of strong boards. Just enough room for him to hide.

As he hops over the lip of the well, he hears Rachel calling. He tries to keep in a laugh, covering his mouth . . . but his shoulders are vibrating, his whole body is . . .

CRRRACK!

Beneath him, the boards sag and break. His laugh becomes a scream as he plunges into the darkness.

He lands hard. The bottom is damp and rocky, and his leg throbs with pain. For a moment he hears nothing but his own tortured groan and Rachel's far-away scream for help — and something else. Something closer and directly above him. A frenzy of muffled squealing and odd, papery slaps. Sitting up, fighting the pain, Bruce squints up into the circle of light.

There is a hint of movement among the stones, a jerky flutter.

From a gash in the wall comes an explosion of black. It billows like a cloud, blotting out the light. It is inky and alive, and in its depths are angry eyes, teeth like needles. It descends toward him — jittering, scolding, shrieking.

As claws rip into his hair, Bruce curls himself into a ball. And he screams. . . .

The image dissolves into a fracture of electric jolts.

The next thing he sees is a swirl of brown, the carved oak walls of the Wayne Manor grand staircase. He is gliding upward in his father's strong, familiar arms. The only sound is the tread of his father's footfalls on the Persian rug. He sees the pale, stricken faces of Rachel and Mrs. Dawes in the light of the crystal chandelier. Alfred, Father's manservant, walks alongside.

In a moment Bruce feels the mattress beneath

him. Mother stands in the doorway, her eyes moist and concerned. "He'll be fine," Father says, his calm voice soothing. "I'll set the broken bone. I've ordered X-rays."

Bruce is not aware of falling asleep, but when his eyes open next it is darker. He is alone with Alfred, who is reaching for the window curtains. "Took quite a fall, didn't we?" Alfred says. It is twenty years ago and his graying hair is still streaked with brownish-red. His cockney accent is lighter, younger. "And why do we fall, Master Bruce?"

Bruce winces. He knows the answer but he can't possibly recite it now.

"So that we might better learn to pick ourselves up," Alfred says with a patient smile, pulling the curtains shut.

The blue poppy was not hard to find. On the easternmost slope, exactly where Ducard had said, a field of poppies stretched to the horizon.

Bruce picked one and looked up toward the mountain's icy peak, shrouded by clouds. Only a fool would attempt such a climb without sophisticated gear, warm clothing, food, and a team of fellow climbers. It would be insanity. Certain suicide.

Fastening the poppy to his ragged tunic, Bruce began walking.

With each mile, each ten-degree temperature drop, each jab of rock into the soles of his feet, Bruce felt farther — not closer — to the top. It felt like weeks before he reached a hamlet tucked into the mountain slope. His cold hands shaking, he approached the villagers but they fled. A child, his face unforgiving, pointed to the poppy pinned to Bruce's tunic. "No one will help you," he said.

Wordlessly Bruce continued upward.

The timberline was soon behind him, and the snowfall raged unobstructed. In the thinning air, the cold bit like wolf's teeth. Bruce lost feeling in his fingers, then in his ears and cheeks. His lips, although protected by ice clinging to his scraggly beard, became rigid. He staggered and fell, his toes numb. The wind mocked him, pelting him with snow like a sandstorm. He thought of Arctic explorers who had taken a hammer to their frostbitten toes and knocked them off one by one.

Purpose.

He stood on deadened legs, propelling himself by sheer force of will, fighting back tears that streamed down his cheeks and instantly froze. He moved without feeling or sight, nearly blinded by the glare, vowing that death would take him upright, not prone.

He did not see the monastery at first. The only hint of its presence was a shift in the wind's shriek, a bending of pitch that could only have been caused by something large in his path.

Staggering forward on momentum alone, Bruce pitched headfirst into a thick oaken door. He moved his arms in a pounding motion, producing only a feeble thump of frozen flesh upon wood.

The door groaned, slowly swinging open.

A rush of color and heat pulled him inside, and he stumbled through a corridor lit with flickering lamps.

Blinking against the sting of sudden warmth, he saw a robed figure seated atop a platform. The man's head was shaved, his sharp features calm and focused. "Rā's al Ghūl?" Bruce rasped.

A phalanx of ninja warriors stepped from the shadows, bows and swords primed. Shaking, Bruce unhooked the blue poppy and held it out.

Rā's al Ghūl began to speak in a language Bruce recognized as Urdu . . . but it was Ducard, stepping into the light, who translated: "Fear has been your guide. It will keep you on your knees. We will help you conquer your fear. In exchange you will renounce the cities of man. You will live in solitude. You will be a member of the League of Shadows, and you will be without fear." Ducard took the flower and inserted it into his lapel. "Are you ready to begin?"

Bruce fought the urge to collapse. "Ready? I . . . I can barely —"

Ducard kicked Bruce to the floor. "Death does not wait for you to be ready. Death is not considerate or fair. Make no mistake — today death is your opponent."

Bruce gasped, trying to regain his breath. Holding fast to the last glimmer of life in his body, he rose.

Ducard struck again. By force of will, by sense memory alone, Bruce responded — his arm blocked a kick, his leg lashed out. Thrust, parry, strike.

"Jujitsu?" Ducard mocked. "This is not a dance." He attacked like an animal now — fierce and messy, connecting with Bruce's cheek, midsection, chin. "Facing death, you learn the truth. You are weak . . . you are alone . . . and you are afraid. . . ."

Bruce slumped to the floor, but he would not give in to a beating. Never. Fighting pain, he glared into Ducard's face.

"You are not afraid of me," Ducard said, bemused. He pulled the flower from his lapel and placed it on Bruce's chest. "Tell us, Wayne . . . what *do* you fear?"

Bruce tried to answer, but his mind now drifted in and out of unconsciousness, until he wasn't sure what he was dreaming and what he was saying. . . .

It is a winter night. When he awakens from sleep, it is dark and he is screaming.

He has visited the well again. . . .

His father rushes in, wrapped in his dressing gown. "The bats?" he asks, sitting on the bed.

Bruce nods, relieved. He is embarrassed to have disturbed Father.

"You know why they attacked you?" Father asks, smoothing Bruce's hair. "Because they were afraid of

you. You're a lot bigger than a bat, aren't you? All creatures feel fear."

"Even the scary creatures?" Bruce asks.

"Especially the scary ones." Father reaches into his pocket. "Here, let me show you something — but you can't tell anyone, right?"

He pulls out a jewel case and opens it to reveal a string of perfect pearls. "For your mother," he says with a wink.

Bruce grins. It will be their secret. Tomorrow night is Mother's birthday. He can already see the smile on her face.

Jewels. From the train window the next evening, the city looks like a forest of jewels. They are going to the opera, which Bruce doesn't like. But the train ride, as always, is a treat. His father built this entire system. His great-grandfather, who established Wayne Industries, had built Gotham's very first trains. Bruce feels proud. He loves the city. It's like a human body, breathing, shouting, growing, always moving. The train system circles around it, with branches flowing inward like veins and sinew and nerves.

They stop under the vaulted glass ceiling of Wayne Station. Everything — even the great tower that rises above them — seems to bear the name WAYNE. "The city's been good to our family," Father has always said. "It was time to give something back."

If only they could give back the opera house . . .

Actually, at first he doesn't mind the performance. There are witches around a cauldron and cool, creepy music.

But the bats take Bruce by surprise.

They burst from a crevice on the stage — wings flapping, teeth flashing. They are fake, FAKE, but it doesn't matter. His head is light, his heart pounding. The claws . . . HE CAN FEEL THE CLAWS. . . .

He grabs his father's arm. "Can we go?"

Father understands right away. He rises, holding Bruce's hand — and the three of them make their way to the aisle. They push their way through a side exit.

"Bruce, what's wrong?" Mother asks as they step

into a dark alleyway. She doesn't understand the fear, and Bruce is too ashamed to admit it.

"I just needed a bit of air, Martha," Father pipes up. "A bit of opera goes a long way – right, Bruce?"

Bruce is grateful for his father's excuse. He looks up, and Father winks. Together they head up the alley toward the sidewalk.

They are cut off by a man in the shadows. A beggar, Bruce thinks – until he sees the reflection of streetlight on the barrel of a gun. "Wallet, jewelry!" the man screams. "Fast!"

Bruce freezes. His knees are rigid.

"That's fine, just take it easy," Father says. Calmly he hands Bruce his coat, then pulls out his wallet and hands it to the man.

The man's hands are shaking, his eyes wild. He drops the wallet, shrieking, "I said jewelry!"

He thrusts his gun toward Mother's neck, touching the pearls. The beautiful pearls. Father steps in front of her quickly. "Hey, just a –"

CRRRRACK!

A sound like a giant firecracker makes Bruce flinch. Father slumps.

"Thomas!" Mother screams, trying to hold him up. "THOMAS!"

Father is on the ground. Something seeps from his chest. Liquid. Blood. It's fanning outward in a pool.

"Give me that necklace —" the man shouts.

CRRRRACK!

His mother lurches, then falls. The man grabs her necklace, but it snaps. The pearls clatter softly to the sidewalk and roll into the shadows.

Bruce stares at his parents without comprehension, not letting in the thought that they are . . .

Dead.

The killer's face is ashen, ringed with sweat. Then he is gone, running out of the alley.

Bruce sinks to his knees. Beside him, pearls fleck the asphalt beside him.

Some of them are glistening red.

The next few days are a blur. There is a detective named Gordon at the police station afterward, who drapes Father's coat over Bruce's shoulders. A police captain — Loeb — yells at Gordon for his kind act and expects Bruce to be happy at his promise to capture the killer.

Richard Earle, Father's second-in-command at Wayne Industries, approaches Bruce at the cemetery and assures him that Wayne Industries will be waiting for Bruce when he grows up.

None of that matters. The guilt preys on him, sapping his energy, his hunger. When Alfred asks about supper that first night, all Bruce can say is, "It was my fault. I made them leave the theater. If I hadn't gotten scared —"

Alfred, whose emotions usually range from restrained cheer to mild disapproval, is red and puffy in the face. "No," he says, wrapping Bruce in an embrace. "Nothing you did — nothing anyone ever did — can excuse that man. It's his fault, and his alone. Do you understand?"

Bruce buries his face in the old man's chest, sobbing. "I miss them, Alfred. I miss them so much!"

"So do I, Master Bruce," Alfred replies in a barely audible voice. "So do I."

They sit there, gently rocking, as the season's first snow swirls past the window.

"You feel responsible for what happened to your parents?" Ducard asked.

They were walking through the monastery now. Bruce struggled to keep himself upright as feeling returned to his toes and fingers. "My anger outweighs my guilt," he replied.

They passed through a mezzanine stacked with boxes and bottles. Robed ninja warriors were carefully pouring powders into small packets. Ducard took a pinch of the powder and threw it to the floor.

BANG! Bruce flinched at the sharp report.

"Advanced techniques of ninjitsu employ explosive powders," Ducard explained. "Used as weapons — or distractions. Theatricality and deception are powerful agents. Flesh and blood, however skilled, can be destroyed. You must be more than just a man in the minds of your opponents."

They continued outside, trudging to the edge of a frozen lake. There, Ducard handed Bruce a sword and a long silver glove festooned with sharp hooks — a protective gauntlet.

They circled each other, the wind blowing harshly in Bruce's ear. The snow had stopped, and Bruce felt strength pouring back into him.

SHHHINK!

Ducard struck first, but Bruce parried with his gauntlet, leaping away.

Below him, the ice cracked.

"Mind your surroundings," Ducard warned. "Always."

Bruce lunged — but Ducard blocked with *his* gauntlet, catching Bruce's thrust in his hooks. "Your parents' death's were not your fault," he said, wrenching the sword from Bruce's grip and flinging it away. "It was your father's. He failed to act."

The comment reached into a place *no one* was allowed. Bruce leaped at Ducard's throat — but Ducard ducked away, grabbing Bruce by his tunic. "The man had a gun!" Bruce growled.

"The will to take control is everything," Ducard said. "Your father trusted his city, its logic. He thought he understood the attacker and could simply give him what he wanted."

No, thought Bruce. *Father was kind and understanding. Accommodating. It wasn't his fault.*

He pushed away from Ducard. The two men faced each other, their breaths puffing small white clouds. "Your father did not understand the forces of decay," Ducard continued. "Cities like Gotham are in their death throes — chaotic, grotesque, beyond saving."

"Beyond saving?" Bruce asked. "You believe that?"

Ducard gazed out over the stark whiteness of the landscape. "It is not right that one must come so far to see the world as it is meant to be — pure, serene, solitary. These are the qualities we hold dear. But the important thing is whether *you* believe it. Can

Gotham be saved, or is she an ailing ancestor whose time has run out?"

With a sudden motion, Ducard struck with his sword. Bruce blocked the thrust, dropped to the ice, and slid . . . between Ducard's legs, to the place where his sword had fallen. . . .

Bruce clutched the sword and swung a low, swift blow at Ducard's feet.

Ducard jumped, but not quickly enough, slipping to the ice. Bruce stood over him, touching the tip of his sword to Ducard's throat. "Yield," he said.

"You haven't beaten me. You've sacrificed sure footing for a killing stroke." Calmly Ducard tapped his sword near Bruce's feet.

Bruce heard a crack beneath him — and he fell through the surface, into the black water beneath.

5

Bruce rubbed his arms briskly over a fire Ducard had built at the frozen lake's shore. "You have strength born of years of grief and anger, Wayne," Ducard said. "The strength of a man denied revenge. Why could you not avenge your parents?"

It was a good question, but Bruce had no answer. Only memories . . .

The train pulls into Wayne Station. Bruce is twenty now, a dozen years older than he was on the awful day. Bitterness has encased him like armor. No college, thus far, has been able to hold him — or tolerate him. No matter. Alfred has arranged for Rachel Dawes to pick him up this afternoon at Wayne

Manor. She is now assistant district attorney. Together they will attend the parole release hearing for his parents' killer, a two-bit criminal named Joe Chill. Bruce has a plan that will seal both Chill's fate and his own.

Wayne Station has changed over the years. Although it is morning, the filth on the broken glass skylight casts the place in darkness. The walls are cracked and defaced. Homeless people huddle on the floor. Bruce fights a pang of sadness — but he is not surprised.

He walks toward the Red Line transfer, but Alfred is on the platform. "You didn't have to pick me up," Bruce says, shaking the old man's hand.

"Well, sir, the Red Line . . . it's closed," Alfred says, taking Bruce's bag. "Apparently Mr. Earle thought it wasn't making enough money."

Bruce nods. He'd never liked Earle, even as a boy.

As they approach Wayne Manor, Bruce feels hatred for the brooding hulk of a house. The feeling mounts as he and Alfred ascend the stairs, surrounded by furniture hidden under sheets. "You will be in the master bedroom, of course," Alfred says. "It is, after all, your house."

Bruce recoils at the thought of staying in his parents' room. "This isn't my house, Alfred. It's a mausoleum. A reminder of everything I lost. When I have my way, I'll pull the thing down brick by brick."

Alfred turns. It is the first time Bruce has ever seen him angry. "This house, Master Wayne, has sheltered six generations of the Wayne family. It has stood by patiently while you've cavorted in and out of a dozen private schools and colleges. As have I. The Wayne family legacy is not so easily shrugged off."

Bruce nods. His anger fades in the harsh light of Alfred's glare. "Nor borne, old friend," he says softly. "I'm sorry to have disappointed you."

"Master Wayne," Alfred replies, "I was at your father's side when you were born, and at your side when he was laid to rest. Your father was a great man, but I have every confidence that you will exceed his greatness."

Thinking of his plan, Bruce cringes. "Haven't given up on me yet?" he asks.

Alfred's answer is instant and unwavering. "Never."

Alone in his bedroom, Bruce lifts a gun from his valise. If everything works, he will need only one shot.

When he hears a car pull up, he lowers the gun. It's Rachel. She has golden brown hair and a smile that the years have only improved. Was she this beautiful when she was a girl? How could he not have noticed?

He tucks his gun away and runs down to meet her. "You look well," he says, stepping outside. "Assistant district attorney, right?"

Rachel nods. "You still trying to get kicked out of the entire Ivy League?"

"It turns out you don't need a degree to do the international playboy thing."

Rachel smiles uncertainly. "I don't suppose I can convince you not to come? We all loved your parents, and what Chill did is unforgivable —"

"Then why is your boss letting him go?" Bruce shoots back.

"Because in prison he shared a cell with Carmine Falcone," Rachel replies. "He learned things, and he'll testify in exchange for early parole."

A deal. This was how Gotham was run now, in the post-Wayne era of decay and lawlessness. Gifts under the table. One hand washing the other.

Silently Bruce opens the car door and slips inside. His secret burns inside him, but Rachel is the last person he can confide in.

At the courthouse, she leaves the car first. Bruce quietly opens his door and hides the gun under the front wheel. It will be safe there from metal detectors.

He joins Rachel as she heads inside the building and down a corridor. In a small judicial chamber, he sits among scattered observers. Before a grim, five-person panel stands Joe Chill.

Bruce works to unclench his fist.

Rachel's boss, District Attorney Finch, is a pasty-faced man who addresses the panel in a monotone: "Given the exemplary prison record of Mr. Chill, the years already served, and his cooperation with one of this office's most important investigations, we endorse Mr. Chill's petition for early release."

The panel's chairman nods. "I gather a member of the Wayne family is here today? Does Mr. Wayne have anything to say?"

Chill stiffens. As he turns, Bruce sees his aging, prison-hardened face. Chill is now older than his father ever lived to be.

Bruce rises. Silently he leaves the building. Heading straight to Rachel's car, he takes his gun and tucks it into his sleeve. When Chill emerges from a side entrance, flanked by cops and reporters, Bruce moves. Quickly.

"It's Bruce Wayne!" a reporter cries out.

His breaths come hard now. He reaches up his sleeve.

"Joe! Hey, Joe!" a blond TV reporter screams. She is running toward Chill, right in Bruce's path, reaching into a shoulder bag. "Falcone says hi!"

In her hand is a gun. She thrusts it into Joe Chill's chest and fires.

Bruce is numb as Rachel's car speeds along the freeway above Gotham. He cannot comprehend what has just happened. "All these years I wanted to kill Chill," Bruce says. "Now I can't. He killed my parents. They deserved justice."

"You're not talking about justice!" Rachel argues, appalled. "You're talking about revenge. Justice is about harmony. Revenge is about you making yourself feel better. That's why we have an impartial system."

"Well, your system of justice is broken —"

"Don't you tell me the system's broken, Bruce!" Rachel cuts in. "I'm out here every day trying to fix it, while you mope around using your grief as an excuse to do nothing."

Rachel swerves, taking an exit ramp into a neighborhood Bruce barely recognizes. Years ago, working people lived here — shopkeepers, waiters, plumbers, dentists. Now those streets are rutted, the buildings boarded up. Now hollowed-eyed people sit on the stoops as shady young men do deals in street corner shadows. "You care about justice?" Rachel continues. "Look beyond your own pain, Bruce. This city is rotting. Chill is not the cause, he's the effect. Corruption is killing Gotham. Chill's death makes it worse, because Falcone walks. He carries on, flooding our city with crime and drugs – creating new Joe Chills. Falcone may not have killed your parents, Bruce, but he's destroying everything they stood for."

She drives straight to the Gotham Harbor docks, stopping near an unmarked door. Music wafts up from a basement club as a bouncer eyes them threateningly.

"They all know where to find Falcone," Rachel says, gesturing to the club, "but no one will touch him, because he keeps the bad people rich and the good people scared. What chance does Gotham have when the good people do nothing?"

"I'm not one of your 'good people,' Rachel. Chill took that from me." Bruce shows her his gun up his sleeve. "I was going to kill him myself."

Rachel blanches. Then she rears back and slaps

him, tears streaming down her face. "You're no better than the rest. Your father would be ashamed of you!"

Bruce cannot stay in the car. He opens the door and steps out, heading toward the river. He doesn't turn as Rachel drives off, instead walking along the docks, where ship lights glide across the black river. He takes out his gun, watching the light play against the barrel. Then, with a vicious heave, he flings it into the water. He won't need it now. He has a new plan. One that involves Falcone. A deal.

Bruce approaches the club, taking out a wad of money. The bouncer is bought off with half — and a promise of the rest when he signals that Falcone is leaving.

From a hiding place in the shadows, Bruce waits until three men swagger out of the door. One is rich and ruthless; the other two are thugs.

"'Night, Mr. Falcone!" the bouncer calls out as they head toward a waiting limo.

Bruce moves fast, keeping to the shadows. The first thug goes down with a kick to the head, the other with a sharp flip to the ground.

"The little rich kid," Falcone says, eyeing Bruce with amusement. "No gun? I'm insulted."

"I don't need a gun."

Falcone smiles. "Yes, you do."

Bruce feels the cold edge of a pistol at his temple. At the other end is the bouncer.

"Money isn't power down here," Falcone says. "Fear is."

Bruce feels a sharp blow and falls in agony. The bouncer drops Bruce's money onto his chest.

Falcone stands over him. "You don't belong down here, kid. We don't play fair. You miss your mommy and daddy? Come down here again, I'll send you to them."

In a moment the limo is gone. Bruce struggles to his feet and staggers along the docks. Three tough youths approach — but they swerve to avoid him.

"No one will mess with you," calls a homeless guy, warming himself by a flaming oil drum. He points to Bruce's tailored cashmere coat. "If you wander 'round here dressed like that, it means you got something to prove. A man with something to prove is dangerous."

Bruce thinks about that for a moment — image makes the man. He eyes the dock, where workers load cargo onto a freighter about to depart. Quickly taking the wad of money from his wallet, Bruce hands it to the homeless guy. "This is for your jacket."

As the shocked man removes his raggedy coat Bruce hands him the money. Then he drops his wallet — and his tie — into the fire. From tonight onward, he will cease being Bruce Wayne, International Playboy. He has work to do. Things to learn. He will need to start at the bottom.

He exchanges coats. Then he sneaks onto the freighter.

The ceremony took place in the monastery throne room. Bruce wore a black ninja uniform, as did Ducard.

In a pestle on the altar, Ducard ground Bruce's poppy, now dried to paper-thinness. Carefully he poured the dust into a small burner and lit it. "Drink in your fears," Ducard said as the smoke rose in silvery wisps. "Face them."

Bruce inhaled the foul smoke. It seeped in, seeming to spread behind his eyes, and he began seeing things. . . .

Smoke . . . Chill's cold, confused eyes looking

down at his parents' bodies . . . himself plunging down
the well . . . Father falling to the pavement. . . .

Bruce shook his head, making the memories disperse. Ducard put on a ninja mask and motioned for Bruce to do the same. Around them ninjas stepped out of the shadows — dozens of them, identically masked and cloaked. "To conquer fear, you must *become* fear," said Ducard, now lost in the multitude. "You must bask in the fear of other men . . . and men fear most what they cannot see."

He lunged away from the crowd, striking hard. Bruce spun and parried, but Ducard was gone. The ninjas, like a moving curtain, advanced from all directions. "It is not enough to be a man," Ducard called out. "You must become an idea. A terrible thought. A *wraith*."

A glint of steel swooshed to his right.

Bruce leaped away from Ducard's blade. Toward the others. He wanted to blend in with *them*, give Ducard a taste of his own terror . . . but his sleeve had been shredded by Ducard's sword. The ripped fabric would give away his identity. He crouched behind the wall of robes, thinking, fighting the drug-induced images that invaded his mind again . . . *the darkness . . . the well. . . .*

The human wall parted to reveal a box of polished oak.

"*Face your fear. . . .*" Ducard's voice was distant, ghostly. Bruce approached the box and carefully lifted the lid.

WHOOOOSH. Hundreds of bats burst upward, shrieking, dripping venom, clawing at Bruce's face. He leaped away, stifling a scream. *NO! DON'T LET THEM . . .*

Ducard leaped from the wall, sword aloft.

Bruce dropped and rolled behind the wall of warriors again, fighting to hold on to reality but seeing the bats everywhere. He lashed out at them with his sword. . . .

SHHHHSST. He accidentally slashed the sleeve of a ninja.

Yes. That's it. He knew what he needed to do next. Raising his sword, he slashed again and again, with careful aim.

Not far away, in the center of the crowd, Ducard searched for a sign of his prey. When he found a telltale ripped sleeve, he knocked the robed man to the ground. "Become one with the darkness, Bruce Wayne," he said, placing his sword to the cloaked throat. "You cannot leave any sign."

A voice behind him replied, "I haven't."

Ducard whirled around in surprise. Facing him were dozens of other ninjas whose sleeves Bruce had slashed. He had the wrong man. Bruce had fooled him.

As the ninjas turned and sat, Ducard led Bruce to the altar. Before Rā's al Ghūl, they sat on either side of a bottle and a burning candle. Ducard poured Bruce a glass of dark liquid, translating as Rā's al Ghūl spoke: "We have purged your fear. You are ready to lead these men. You are ready to become a member of the League of Shadows. Drink."

Bruce downed the liquid and nearly gagged.

"By blowing out this candle," Ducard continued, "you renounce your mortal life. You renounce forever the cities of man. You dedicate your life to solitude."

Bruce leaned forward obediently, then stopped, eyeing the sea of silent disciples. "Where will I be leading these men?"

"To Gotham," Ducard replied. "You yourself are a victim of Gotham's decay. That is why you came here, and that is why you must go back. You will assume the mantle of your birthright. As Gotham's favored son, you will be ideally placed."

"For what?" Bruce asked

"To help us destroy the city."

"*What?*" This had to be a trick. It was too twisted to be real.

Ducard continued to translate Rā's al Ghūl's speech: "When Gotham falls, the other cities will follow. Nature's balance will be restored, and man will finally return to solitude."

"*You* can't believe in this," Bruce said to Ducard.

"Rā's al Ghūl has rescued you from the darkest corner of your own heart," Ducard replied. "What he asks in return is obedience, and the courage to do what is necessary."

Obedience.

This was the end result of his test, his years of struggle and exile – to destroy what his family had built? The work of his father and mother, and his great-grandfather?

Bruce unsheathed his sword. Leaping to his feet, he smashed the bottle and tipped the candle to the floor.

The fire ignited the wood planks and began to spread.

"What are you doing?" Ducard exclaimed.

"What's necessary." Bruce struck Ducard in the head with the butt of his sword, then ripped off his mask. Setting it aflame, he tossed it high – into the mezzanine where the explosive powders were stored.

Rā's al Ghūl himself leaped from his throne.

BOOOOM!

The first explosion belched flame as Rā's al Ghūl attacked, wielding his sword furiously.

BOOOOM! BOOOOM! BOOOOM!

Fire exploded around them, broken wood and glass flying like shrapnel. Ninjas leaped to the floor, engulfed in fire. With a loud crack, a section of the roof tumbled toward them.

Bruce leaped away – but Rā's al Ghūl was crushed.

Bruce carried the inert Ducard through the entrance passage, out the front door, and onto the frozen slope.

Behind them the building erupted in a blazing fireball. Bruce fell, grabbing onto a rock outcropping – but the unconscious Ducard spun toward the edge of a cliff.

Bruce scrambled after him. As Ducard's body went over, Bruce grabbed onto him firmly. With his other arm, he struck downward with his gauntlet, digging into the ice with his metal hooks. They held fast – but how much weight would they support? Bruce pulled the limp Ducard up . . . up . . .

And over.

Planting his boots, Bruce dragged Ducard away from the edge.

The walk down the slope was not as painful as the walk up. Bruce left Ducard in the small Sherpa hamlet he had seen on his ascent, at the hut of an old man.

"I will tell him you saved his life," the man said.

"Tell him I have an ailing ancestor who needs me," Bruce replied, before beginning his long journey home.

7

Bruce looked out the window of the Wayne private jet as it circled Gotham. He felt, as always, grateful to Alfred. He'd received Bruce's phone call and instantly had flown to Bhutan in the Wayne private G5.

During the flight, Bruce had learned of Gotham's descent into decay and corruption. Falcone, more than anyone else, ran the city. He was rumored to control Judge Faden, Gotham's highest-ranking magistrate.

Wayne Industries, now a weapons and defense contractor, was controlled by Mr. Earle, who had declared Bruce Wayne legally dead. He planned to take the company public, turning it over to stock-holders and collecting a bundle.

The Gotham River circled the city like a jeweled necklace in the sun. But Bruce's eyes were riveted on Wayne Tower, a bit more soot-stained but still proud. It looked different to him now, as if he'd discovered a missing part of himself. "Alfred," he said, "no one can know I'm back yet. I'll need everything on the company – shareholders' reports, holdings, every-thing."

"You sound like a man with a purpose," Alfred said cheerfully.

"Gotham needs me, Alfred," Bruce replied. "Gotham needs a symbol."

"What . . . *symbol,* sir?"

It is not enough to be a man, Ducard had said. *You must become an idea . . . a wraith.* "Something for the good to rally behind," Bruce replied, "and the criminals to fear. . . ."

As Bruce watched the TV news at Wayne Manor, he spotted a fluttering shadow on the ceiling. Behind him, Alfred entered with a tea service. "A bat again, sir," he explained. "They nest somewhere on the grounds."

Bruce's eyes followed the helpless, trapped creature. How could something so small have frightened him so? Being afraid of a bat was like being scared of a shadow. A ghost.

A wraith.

Bruce bolted from the sofa and into the foyer, leaving Alfred slack-jawed. He grabbed a long overcoat and then ran outside to the equipment shed, where he gathered a long rope and a blowtorch. Striding past the greenhouse, now dry and derelict, he reached the old stone well.

He had not come here in many years. Now, securing the rope, he lowered himself down. Memories surrounded him — the fall, the gash in the rocks, the cloud of bats — but he was no longer afraid.

When Bruce reached the bottom, he looked up at the crevice in the wall. What once seemed so high was now only chest level. Pushing himself into the crawlspace, Bruce slid over slick rocks, into a cold, dank wind. At the end, a small chamber sloped downward to blackness. From the darkness came the sound of rushing water.

He slid inside, legs first, and landed on a rocky floor. The water's sound was loud and close. From the pocket of his overcoat he pulled his torch, lit it, and held it aloft. A cavern took shape around him, the walls jagged, the ceiling spiked with stalactites. A river flowed through, traveling into the darkness.

As he moved the torch, he noticed movement in the shadows on the ceiling. Bats – thousands of them. Waking, stretching their wings, lunging toward the light of his torch. Bruce crouched instinctively.

Then, slowly, he stood. The bats surrounded him, flapping, screeching, fierce, restless. But he welcomed them now. He knew in his soul what had *really* scared him as a boy. It was not the animal itself. It was what it represented – the unknown.

The one thing every person feared.

Bruce turned his face toward the squealing mass on the ceiling, and he smiled.

The next morning, dressed in a suit, Bruce smiled his way past the receptionist's protests and barged into the boardroom of Wayne Industries.

Mr. Earle was presiding over a meeting. Sitting near him was Gotham's esteemed Judge Faden. "As responsible managers," Earle said to the judge, "it falls to us to begin a public offering for Wayne Industries in the wake of Bruce Wayne's death, and so we're sure you will see fit that any legal matters —"

"Sorry to barge in," Bruce interrupted, "but I was in the area."

Earle's face went pale. "My boy!" he exclaimed,

forcing a smile and rushing to shake Bruce's hand. "We thought you were gone for good!"

"Actually, I've come to work," Bruce replied. "I thought I'd find out what we actually *do* around here. . . ."

What they did, according to Earle, was start new employees at department level — which was how Bruce ended up at Applied Sciences.

AS had been an important cog in the company's wheel, developing prototypes for many industries. But now its warehouse, once full of cool equipment and an army of technicians, was a cold, empty place stacked with dusty gadgets. It was presided over by a quiet man named Lucius Fox.

"Environmental applications, defense projects, consumer products . . ." Fox gestured wearily. "All prototypes, none in production at any level whatsoever."

"*None?*" Bruce asked.

Fox gave him a bemused look. "I don't know what they told you about this place, but they told me it was a dead end where I couldn't cause any more trouble for the rest of the board."

"You were on the board?"

"Back when your father ran things. I helped him build his train. Beautiful project — routed right into Wayne Tower, along with the water and power utilities. Made Wayne Tower the unofficial heart of Gotham." Fox stopped in front of a tall crate and pulled out a bodysuit made of silicone over jointed armor. "The Nomex survival suit for advanced infantry — Kevlar biweave, reinforced joints. Bulletproof to anything but a straight shot, and tear-resistant. This sucker will stop a knife. But the bean counters figured a soldier's life wasn't worth the three hundred grand."

"I want to borrow it," Bruce said, feeling the suit's fibers. "For spelunking. Cave-diving."

Fox raised an eyebrow. "You get a lot of gunfire down in those caves?"

Bruce smiled. "I'd rather Mr. Earle didn't know about me borrowing this."

"The way I see it," Fox replied, "*all* this stuff is yours, anyway."

That evening, with Alfred holding a lantern, Bruce used his climbing gear to hammer a string of lamps across the cavern ceiling. When he was done, Alfred flicked on a portable generator. The fixtures threw a dim light from among the cavern crags.

"Oh, *charming*," Alfred drawled, looking up into the mass of bats that covered the ceiling. "At least you'll have company."

Alfred peered at another part of the ceiling where a corner of crumbling reddish brickwork poked through. "Look — must be the lowest foundations of the southeast wing."

Curious, Bruce climbed closer and investigated. The bricks supported a wrought-iron spiral staircase that surrounded a dumbwaiter, a small elevator used to transport goods upward. It had fallen off its track.

"During the Civil War your great-grandfather was involved with the Underground Railroad," Alfred called out, "secretly transporting freed slaves to the North. I suspect these caverns came in handy."

Bruce jumped down. He eyed the river, now dappled with light from the lamps. Where did it go — and what was the faraway roar? He walked along the water's edge. As it curved, the sound grew louder. Out of the lamps' range, a soft light began to bathe the area. Soon the cavern veered sharply right. When Bruce took the turn, he stopped in his tracks.

The river's source was a powerful waterfall. Its billowing skirt was ringed by mist and lined by rock slopes. Grinning, he climbed the rocks for a closer look. "Alfred, come up here!"

"I can see it very well from here, thank you, sir," Alfred replied, standing primly on dry ground.

Bruce laughed. His plans were taking shape. He had a lair, an accomplice, a uniform, a supply depot. . . .

And a symbol.

Bruce knew he'd have to learn, adapt, practice — but when he was finished, he would own the night. He would harness the power of darkness and fear for the good of all.

He would have to move fast.

9

The black Nomex bodysuit felt like another skin. It protected Bruce and hid him in the night. He used his ninja spikes to climb the building wall. On the roof, peering through the eyeholes of his wool mask, he not only could see the cop car parked by the liquor store but he could hear snatches of conversation. One officer was a middle-aged guy named Flass who had the cocky grin of a cop on the take. The other man was unmistakable – Gordon, the detective who had been so thoughtful on the night of his parents' murder. Gordon was grayer and heavier now – and from the looks of things, a sergeant.

Flass made no effort to hide the money he'd

collected from the store owner. Climbing into the car, he offered half to Gordon.

But Gordon wasn't in. Bruce could read the disdain on his face. There were still good people in Gotham. Bruce would need to count on them.

He followed the car to the precinct house, then scaled the building's wall to Gordon's window. Slipping in, he hid behind a file cabinet until the sergeant returned. As Gordon slumped into his chair, Bruce jammed the nose of a stapler between the sergeant's shoulders — a bluff, and the only foolproof way to prevent him from turning.

Gordon put his hands up. "What do you want?"

"I've been watching," Bruce replied. "You're a good cop. One of the few. What would it take to get Carmine Falcone? He brings in shipments of drugs every week, yet nobody takes him down. Why?"

Gordon shrugged. "He's paid up with the right people. To get him, it would take leverage on Judge Faden. And a DA brave enough to prosecute."

"That would be Rachel Dawes, Finch's assistant. Watch for a sign."

"Who are you?" Gordon demanded. "Are you just one man?"

"Now we are two," Bruce said, and without a sound, he left — out the window and up onto the roof.

Move. He ran to the rooftop ledge and eyed the gap to the next building. Too wide. Behind him, footsteps clattered on the stairwell to the roof. "FREEZE!" a voice commanded.

Gordon.

Bruce leaped over the edge. Plummeting, he shifted his body weight, leaning forward, reaching out — it would be close. . . .

His fingers brushed against the next roof ledge and missed.

He dropped straight down, flailing his arms. His hand gripped the railing on the balcony below, but it broke loose and he swung inward, toward the building.

He landed with a thump on the next balcony. Alive . . . and lucky.

Before the sergeant could open fire, Bruce used his ninja spikes to scale the wall around the side of the building, where he dropped into the shadows and out of sight.

Bruce hadn't been to the wharf in years, but it looked the same. Even some of the same homeless people were there. Dressed in rags, Bruce warmed his hands over their fire.

Across the alley, most of the same people were in the club. When Judge Faden emerged and entered a limousine, Bruce ran to it and knocked loudly on the rear window.

"Get lost!" the driver bellowed, kicking Bruce away.

"Leave him alone!" cried a homeless man, who Bruce immediately recognized, from the cashmere coat he'd once given him.

As the limo drove off, Bruce nodded thanks, then glanced at the small digital camera in his left hand.

The image of Faden leaving the club was crystal clear.

Walking to work the next morning, Bruce mentally went over his progress: Two ninja gauntlets sprayed black. From Singapore, a formfitting cowl for the face. From China, spikes that resembled bats' ears. With Alfred's help, the shipments were arriving and the uniform would be perfect. But he still needed to fine-tune, to procure a few more gadgets, so that what happened at the precinct house would not happen again. For that kind of equipment, he counted on Fox.

In the Applied Sciences office, Fox gave him a wry look. "What is it today, more spelunking?"

"Base-jumping," Bruce said. "Like parachuting. I need a lightweight grappling hook. For climbing. See, base-jumping's illegal. You can't just take the elevator."

"We've got suction pads, grapples . . . and this thing's pretty neat." From a box, Fox pulled out a bronze contraption with a shoulder harness and belt. "Air-powered grappling gun. Magnetic grapple. Monofilament tested to three hundred fifty pounds.

But too expensive for the army. Guess they never thought about marketing to the billionaire base-jumping, spelunking market."

Bruce took it. It was lighter than he expected, and exactly what he needed.

"Look, Mr. Wayne," Fox said sharply, "if you don't tell me what you're really doing, then when I get asked I don't have to lie. But don't treat me like an idiot."

Bruce nodded. "Fair enough."

Fox headed for the door. "Come on, I'll show you something."

They walked out to a loading dock, where Fox lifted a sheet of black fabric from a crate. "Memory fabric." From the same crate he took a glove and slipped it onto his hand. Small electrodes protruded from the glove's fingers. "The fabric has dual-layer polymers with variable alignment molecules – flexible ordinarily, but if you put a current through it, the molecules align and become rigid."

He grabbed the fabric with the gloved hand – and it instantly popped into the shape of a small tent. "It could be tailored to any structure based on a rigid skeleton," Fox continued.

Bruce felt its strength. It was impressive. And potentially very useful. But Bruce was distracted by the sight of a vehicle with enormous tires, covered by a tarp. "What's that?" he asked.

"The Tumbler? Oh, you wouldn't be interested in *that*. . . ."

Right.

In moments, Bruce was taking Fox for a high-speed spin along a test track. *Car* was too mundane a word for the vehicle. It looked like a cross between a Lamborghini Countach and a Humvee and drove like a dream. To the right of the usual driving position was a glass-bubble-enclosed cockpit with separate controls and video panels. Bruce used the controls to push the vehicle to its limits.

"She was built as a bridging vehicle!" Fox said from the passenger seat, shouting over the engine noise. He pointed to a button on the center panel. "You hit that and it will boost her into a rampless jump. In combat, two of them jump a river, towing

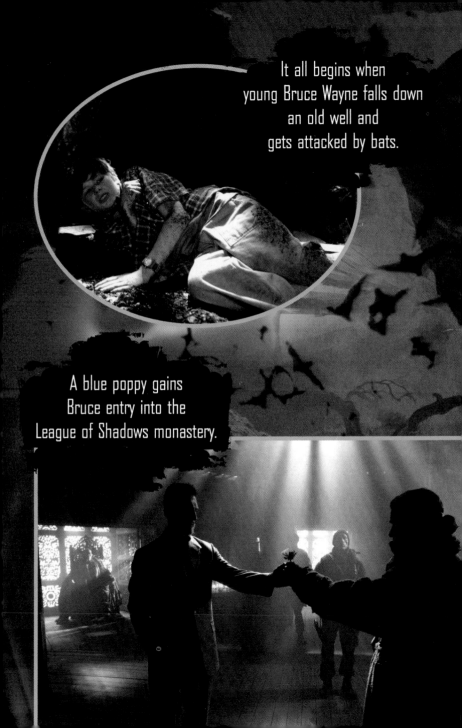

It all begins when
young Bruce Wayne falls down
an old well and
gets attacked by bats.

A blue poppy gains
Bruce entry into the
League of Shadows monastery.

The Batcave is a perfect natural hideout underneath Wayne Manor.

In the Applied Sciences office, Lucius Fox shows Bruce the amazing memory fabric.

The Scarecrow's visions can destroy people's minds.

A fiery escape from the Scarecrow.

Batman must get Rachel Dawes out of Arkham Asylum before the damage from the deadly gas becomes permanent.

Only the Batmobile can use the Batcave's back entrance.

Alfred helps Bruce
escape from the inferno
in Wayne Manor.

Looking for danger?
Try being dragged across
the city by a runaway
monorail train!

A bittersweet farewell amidst the burnt ruins of Bruce's mansion.

Lieutenant Gordon sends out the new signal for Gotham City's hero of the night.

cables, then you run a bailey bridge across. The bridge never worked, but this baby works fine!"

After a few more turns, Bruce brought the Tumbler to a squealing, sudden halt.

"Well," Fox said, looking a little queasy, "what do you think?"

"Does it come in black?" Bruce asked.

The Tumbler was the last ingredient. Now for the final details.

In the cavern, Bruce cut the shoulder straps off the grappling gun's harness, leaving a utility belt with sliding attachments. He slipped on Fox's electric-contact gloves, then the memory-fabric gloves. Onto each finger he'd attached memory-fabric ribbons – which shot out to form extensions like the skeleton of a bat's wing.

The black graphite-alloy cowl fit perfectly over his face and looked more chilling than the wool mask. A servo-mounted microphone fit exactly into one of the spike-shaped ears that had arrived from China.

He would need a weapon. Something that wasn't necessarily lethal but would leave a marker — a calling card. Using plans he'd drawn up in his head, he went to work on a metal lathe to execute a prototype.

Alfred, his partner in development, curiously examined the shape that was taking form. "Why the design, Master Wayne?"

Bruce lifted the steel shank, now curved into a rough boomerang that resembled a bat with extended wings. "A man, however strong, however skilled, is just flesh and blood. I need to be more than a man. I need to be a symbol."

"Why the symbol of the bat?" Alfred asked.

"Bats frighten me. And it's time my enemies shared my dread." Bruce tilted the boomerang into the light, then threw it.

He and Alfred watched as it sliced through the air, whistling around the cavern on its maiden voyage.

10

He was a creature of the night now. A new person, with a new name.

His uniform and utility belt were in place. He had learned every hidden corner of the Gotham dock.

From high in the warehouse's metal supports, he watched a cop approach a team of dockworkers.

Flass. Of course he was in on it.

The cop pulled a toy from an open box in a huge metal ship container. Laughing, he handed it to the workers and continued on to the shipping office.

Not dockworkers. Thugs.

Not a toy. A packet of illegal drugs.

Not a shipping office. Falcone's base of operations.

Bruce knew it all. He'd done his research. A drug deal, Bruce figured — with Falcone the supplier and Flass the enforcer. Someone else was there, too — a middleman, the pond scum who distributed the drugs to the people of Gotham.

As if that weren't enough, Judge Faden was in the backseat of a parked limo in a nearby alleyway.

Begin. Now.

Bruce leaped out of the shadows and onto the limo. The gloves protected his fist as he smashed through the windshield and grabbed the driver. Then, with his free hand, he pressed the dashboard button that lowered the backseat partition.

Faden sat bolt upright.

"You have eaten well, as Gotham has starved," Bruce said, his eyes piercing through the black cowl's slits. "This changes tonight."

The magistrate whimpered in fear — and Bruce leaped onto the roof and away into the wharf's shadows.

Fear.

The first seed had been planted.

Moments later, a dockworker named Schmidt approached a marked shipping container. Steiss, the expediter, handed him a box. The job for Schmidt — and his pals — was to take the box to Falcone. It was heavy, but Schmidt was used to that.

He was *not* used to the scream he heard behind him as he walked away.

When he turned back, Steiss was gone.

Schmidt put the box down and pulled out his gun, inching toward the gaping mouth of the open container. His pals flanked him, guns drawn.

SMMMACK!

To their left, a streetlamp went out.

SMMMACK! SMMMACK! SMMMACK!

All along the wharf, lights exploded. As darkness crept up the dock, Schmidt froze. The lights weren't being *shot* at, he realized. Something was being *thrown* at them. He saw the projectile as it fell to the pavement.

A metal shank in the shape of a bat.

"What the . . . ?" Schmidt grunted.

Overhead something shifted and he looked up. It was a *bat* – a huge one – hanging upside down, wings folded. As it spread its wings, Schmidt caught the glare of two slitted eyes. He didn't have enough time toscream before it dropped, engulfing him in darkness.

In Falcone's office, Dr. Crane sat back in a worn metal chair. He was thin and efficient-looking, with a scholarly European accent. "I'm aware that you're not intimidated by me, Mr. Falcone," he said, adjusting his glasses, "but you know who we're working for. When he gets here, he won't want to hear that you've been endangering our operation just to filch a few dollars from your dealers."

Falcone's thick face twitched. "He's coming to Gotham?"

"Soon," Crane replied. "This is our last shipment."

"Well, then, there's no need to argue. You can just test the stuff here and now." Falcone glared at

Detective Flass, who tossed him a package containing white powder.

"EEAAAAGGHHH!"

A distant scream shattered the night's silence. Falcone reached for his shotgun, and Flass bolted out the door to investigate.

RAT-TA-TA-TA-TA-TA-TAT!

Hearing the sudden blast of machine-gun fire, Flass ducked behind a stack of shipping containers. Falcone ran up beside him, clutching his shotgun.

Crane, slipping out the office door, disappeared into the night.

After another scream, Falcone ran toward his container — and Flass took the opportunity to jump into his patrol car and drive away.

Shotgun cocked, Falcone crept along the container stacks, alone. The shipment had to be protected at all costs. He rounded a corner to find five of his men in a circle back-to-back, weapons in hand, waiting, tensed.

From the steel beams overhead, a shadow dropped into their midst. It was a man — dressed as a giant *bat* — who avoided their chains and knives, spinning and leaping as if it were a game. . . .

In seconds, with no weapon at all, he took out all five thugs.

As he stood over their inert figures, his cape billowing in the wind, Falcone aimed the shotgun at his head. "What *are* you?"

The man turned. He held out his hand, palm up. In it were two shotgun cartridges. "I'm Batman," he said.

Falcone pulled the trigger.

Click.

Nothing.

He dropped the gun, stunned, as the masked man stepped closer.

After his night at the dock, Bruce went across town and made an entrance through Rachel's window.

She was sleeping fitfully, and he hated to wake her. From his cape pocket he pulled out a stack of photographs. "Rachel Dawes," he said softly.

Rachel sprang up, grabbing a taser gun from her dresser.

But Bruce calmly tossed the photos on the bed – images of Judge Faden leaving Falcone's club.

"What is this?" Rachel demanded.

"Leverage," Bruce replied. "To get things moving."

"*Who are you?*"

"Someone like you. Someone who'll stand against the corruption."

Rachel turned to flick on her lamp. When she turned back, he was gone.

Across town, Sergeant Gordon stared in awe at the scene at the dock — Falcone's thugs, unconscious, tied up, and sitting against a shipping container full of drugs. A line of cops held back the press photographers.

"Falcone's men?" asked a beat cop.

Gordon shrugged. "Does it matter? We'll never tie him to it, anyway."

"I wouldn't be too sure of that," the cop replied, pointing upward.

Gordon followed his gesture to a huge harbor light, beaming over the river. Strapped to the searchlight's enormous lens was Falcone — unconscious, arms stretched outward. His sleeves had been ripped in a jagged pattern.

The light's beam left its impression on a cloud: a circle of light, surrounding the silhouette of a bat.

11

Rachel tossed a newspaper onto District Attorney Finch's desk. The front page showed a photo of Falcone strapped to the light. "Can't bury it now," she said.

Finch looked skeptical. "Maybe so, but there's Judge Faden —"

"I've got Faden covered," she replied. The photos were locked in her office safe.

"And this *bat* they're babbling about. . . . ?"

"Even if these guys will swear in court to being thrashed by a giant bat," she said, "we have Falcone *at the scene*. Drugs, prints, cargo manifest — everything."

Finch thought for a moment. "You're right. Let's get frying."

Rachel smiled.

In the police headquarters bullpen, Sergeant Gordon fought to keep his cool. Commissioner Loeb was angry. "Unacceptable!" he roared, slapping today's paper down in front of his captains, sergeants, and lieutenants. "I don't care who did this to Falcone — get them off the street and off the front page!"

"They say it was one guy," a police captain piped up, "or . . . *thing*."

"They're taking their own drugs and hallucinating — it was some jerk in a costume!" Loeb said.

Gordon raised his hand. Twenty-five years on the force had jaded him, but here was an opportunity to catch a big fish. "This guy did deliver us one of the city's biggest crime lords."

"No one takes the law into their own hands in my city," Loeb replied. "*Understand?*"

Gordon nodded. He understood well. As far as

the Gotham police department was concerned, this caped guy was an outlaw.

As far as Gordon was concerned, the city was lucky to have him.

Across the street, at the county jail, a prison official allowed a young doctor to enter a cell block. Dr. Crane, the director of the Arkham Asylum, was responsible for the commitment of mentally unstable prisoners to his institution, an imposing building on an island in the river known as the Narrows.

As they entered an interview room, the official explained that the prisoner in question had cut his wrists – as usual, probably looking for an insanity plea. He pulled up a seat for Crane and quickly left.

Sitting at a table, dressed in prison scrubs and showing his bandaged wrists, Carmine Falcone smiled. "Doctor Crane, it's too much, the walls are closing in . . . blah, blah, blah!" he said mockingly.

"What do you want?" Crane demanded.

"We got a lot to talk about," Falcone replied. "Such as how you're going to convince me to keep my mouth shut. I know you wouldn't want the cops taking a closer look at the drugs they seized."

Crane narrowed his eyes. "You don't know anything."

"I know about your experiments on the inmates at your nuthouse. I don't get into business with someone without finding out their dirty secrets. Those goons you hired — *I* own them. I own muscle in this town." Falcone leaned forward. "So what's hidden in the drugs I bring in for you, Crane?"

"If he wanted you to know, he'd have told you himself."

He. Falcone was tired of hearing about this mysterious *he.* "I've been smuggling your stuff in for months. He's got something big planned. I want in."

"He'll say we should kill you."

"Even he can't touch me in here. Not in my town."

With a shrug, Crane popped open his briefcase. "Would you like to see my mask?"

Falcone eyed him oddly as Crane pulled out a burlap sack with eye holes, stitching for a mouth, and a plastic breathing tube. "I use it in my experiments. Those crazies, they can't stand it. . . ."

As Crane put on the mask, Falcone murmured, "When did the nut take over the asylum?"

WHOOOOSH. White smoke shot out of Crane's briefcase.

Falcone shoved his chair back, coughing, as the stuff rushed into his nostrils. "They scream and cry . . ." Crane continued.

Through watery eyes, Falcone saw lizard tongues, sharp and forked, flicking out of Crane's mask holes.

". . . much as you're doing now," Crane finished.

Crane was on fire. The whole room was on fire! Falcone let out a piercing scream.

Quickly, Crane stuffed the mask back into his briefcase and snapped it shut. The poison rapidly dissipated into the air. He would be fine — but Falcone's nervous system was toast.

"EEEEAGHHHH!"

The prison official ran to the door at Falcone's scream. "Oh, he's not faking," Crane said gravely, stepping into the hallway. "I'll talk to the judge, see if I can get him moved to the secure wing at Arkham. . . ."

12

Earle was angry. He hadn't counted on the return of the lazy prodigal son to ruin his retirement plans. And now, on top of all that, he'd gotten news that something had gone seriously wrong in the Arctic Ocean.

"The coast guard picked up one of our cargo ships last night," said Rogers, his PR flack. "Heavily damaged. Crew missing. The ship was carrying a prototype weapon — a microwave emitter."

Great. Just great. This machine was big . . . and expensive. Designed for desert warfare, it used focused microwaves to vaporize the enemy's water supply into an instant steam cloud. Any damage to the thing would set the budget back, which was bad news to prospective shareholders. "What about the weapon?" he asked.

"It's missing," Rogers said.

That evening, Bruce Wayne pulled up to the Gotham Plaza Hotel in his new Bugati Veyron. He loved the feel of it. With his father's inheritance, the purchase had been quick and easy.

Finding two beautiful blonds hadn't been hard, either. The valets could barely contain themselves at the sight of the car — or the women.

Alfred had insisted that Bruce do this — ease up on the pushups and mental training, have some fun. *With all your strange nighttime bruises and injuries, and your nonexistent social life,* Alfred had pointed out, *people will wonder what exactly Bruce Wayne does with his time and money.* He was right, of course. Appearances must be upheld — to ward off suspicion.

The dinner engagement was with Earle and his

close associates, Falk and Rowena. Dull company — but to Bruce it was worth the price of admission to see the looks on their faces as he walked in with his two guests.

Halfway through dinner the women simply wandered away — and the conversation turned to the mystery of the masked man.

"He put Falcone behind bars," said Falk, "and now the cops are trying to bring him in — so what does that tell you?"

Bruce forced a scornful look. "A guy who dresses up like a bat clearly has issues. If he's so benevolent, why does he hide his face?"

"Maybe he's protecting the people he cares about from reprisals," suggested Rowena.

Suddenly the restaurant's maître d' sidled up to the table and gestured toward the hotel's infinity-shaped pool — which now contained the two giggling women. "Sir, the pool is for decoration. . . ."

"Well, they're European," Bruce said.

"I'm going to have to ask you to leave," the maître d' replied.

"Earle," Bruce suddenly announced, "I'm buying this hotel. Will you please broker a deal?"

Before Earle could respond, Bruce stood and removed his jacket. "I think we should make some new rules for the pool area, don't you?" he said to the maître d', before making a run for the pool himself.

The plan had worked. No one doubted that Bruce Wayne was a spoiled rich guy. *I could get used to this,* he thought as he waited at the valet stand with the robed, barefooted women.

He hadn't expected to see Rachel Dawes walk up to the restaurant for dinner. The look on *her* face made his heart sink.

She was wearing a sleek dark dress and looked stunning – and stunned. "I . . . I'd heard you were back," Rachel said, eyeing the two women. "Where were you?"

"Oh, kind of all over," Bruce replied nervously as his Bugati pulled up. "You know."

"No, Bruce, I don't know," Rachel replied. "Neither did a lot of people. People who thought you were probably dead. Me, I never quite gave up on you."

"Come on, Bruce!" shouted one of the women from inside the car. "We have some more hotels we want you to buy!"

Bruce cringed. "Rachel . . . that's not me. Inside I'm different. I'm —"

"The same great little kid you used to be?" She poked him softly on the chest. "Bruce, it's not who you are underneath, but what you *do* that defines you."

She turned toward the restaurant, her heels clattering on the pavement.

13

Sergeant Gordon dropped his garbage bag into a Dumpster behind his apartment. He heard distant thunder and turned to go back, but he stopped when he saw Detective Flass leaning against his car.

"How's Barbara? The kid?" Flass asked, stepping forward. "Another one on the way, right? Big responsibility. And when you're on a case like Falcone . . . a lot of time away from home? It's good the case is clear-cut. You'll wrap it up easy."

Gordon's eyes flared. "You come around here making threats — it tells me you're scared."

Flass opened his car door and slipped inside. "Take care of yourself, pal," he said.

As the car roared away, a soft voice in the dark said, "Trouble?"

Gordon looked up, startled, and saw Batman crouching on a ledge. "The scum's getting jumpy because you stood up to Falcone," Gordon said.

"Your partner was at the docks with Falcone," Batman replied. "There was another man, too, testing the drugs."

That seemed odd to Gordon. The dock was a place of transit. Only money was unpacked there, not the drugs themselves. "It wasn't a buy," he remarked. "Why risk opening a package on the docks?"

"Flass knows."

"He won't talk. He moonlights as a low-level enforcer."

"He'll talk to me," promised Batman.

Gordon stepped closer. "Commissioner Loeb set up a task force to catch you. He thinks you're dangerous."

"What do *you* think?" Batman asked.

"I think you're trying to help . . ."

A streak of lightning caught Gordon's attention.

When he looked back, Batman was gone. ". . .but I've been wrong before," he murmured.

Rain fell as Bruce hunched on a fourth-story ledge between buildings on a near-deserted Gotham street. Not Bruce. *Batman.* Always Batman on his missions now.

As Flass approached, gorging himself on food, Batman fired his grappling gun. The wire wrapped around the cop's ankle, pulling him from the ground as he shrieked.

"Who was with Falcone at the docks?" Batman demanded, drawing the detective upward so they were eye to eye.

"I don't know!" Flass yelped.

Batman let him drop three stories and yanked him back up.

"I never knew his name!" Flass screamed. "S-sometimes shipments went to him before they went to the dealers! There was something hidden in the drugs —"

"What?"

"I don't know — *something*! I never went to the drop-off — it's in the Narrows. Cops can't go into the Narrows except in force!"

Bruce leaned in closer. "Batman can."

The island in the Narrows had been a blight on Gotham for years. Crumbling and abandoned, the remains of a public housing project hugged the shoreline. In its midst stood the notorious Arkham Asylum, a towering Gothic fortress with barred windows and broad gables that hinted of bleak attic lockups.

Behind the asylum, built around the monorail supports, was a warehouse. Batman moved along its rain-slick outer walls and entered through a set of vents.

His eyes quickly adjusted to the darkness, and he saw what he'd been seeking — a massive shipping crate. He climbed onto it, prying open the lid. Inside was an industrial machine the size of a small van. A label on its side read WAYNE INDUSTRIES: M−EMIT.42B.

The sudden sound of footsteps made him duck back into the shadows.

Two dockworkers entered, along with a thin man wearing glasses.

"The boss wants you to keep it in the asylum until the time comes, Dr. Crane," the first worker said.

"Fine, leave the body," Crane replied. "Torch the place. No traces."

The workers dragged a human body from a hidden corner and into the center of the room — a customs official with a bullet hole, who had obviously walked in at the wrong time and seen this machine.

The men pushed the crate across the floor and into a freight elevator. On a nod from Crane, one of the men lit a fuse leading to a gasoline-filled bottle — and threw it into the room.

SWWWWIII —

Batman launched a line of cable and snagged the bottle. Quickly putting out the fuse, he pounced from his hiding place. He knocked the gun from one thug's hand, smashing his arm to the ground. The other dockworker went down with an elbow to the neck.

Crane had donned his mask of burlap and thread. He raised his arm, and a puff of smoke billowed out of his sleeve.

Batman staggered backward, coughing, the pungent gas working its way into his nostrils. He'd felt this way before — but where? Crane was changing shape . . . his limbs growing like rubber. Flames began shooting from his mouth as he began spinning. . . .

SMMASSSH!

A bottle made contact with Batman's skull. Liquid coursed down the sides of his costume.

Gasoline.

"Need a light?" Crane asked, tossing a lit cigarette lighter at him.

FFFOOM!

Flames shot upward from his legs, engulfing his body, as Batman lurched for the window.

14

The ground rushed up from below, but Batman couldn't think. His mind was flashing thoughts of Rā's al Ghūl . . . the wooden box . . . bats . . . the monastery in flames . . .

The cloak. The memory fabric.

He activated his gloves — but the mechanism had been damaged. Only one side of the cloak went rigid, but it caught the wind. Ablaze, Batman spun downward. The wing hooked a railing, checking his momentum, and he dropped onto the sidewalk.

As he rolled along the wet pavement, the fire sizzled in the rain. Batman groaned, fighting the visions and the flame that blazed equally. . . .

Batman sprang to his feet, smoke rising from his uniform where the fire had now been extinguished. Summoning what was left of his will, he shot the grappling gun upward and lifted himself onto a roof, out of sight.

Reaching into his cape for his cell phone, Batman punched in a number and groaned, "Alfred . . . come . . . poisoned . . . need a blood sample. . . ."

The opera house was back again . . . the bats blackening the stage . . . he saw himself saying, "We have to go now, Dad!" . . . *NO!*

Bruce shivered, opening his eyes from the nightmare. He was home, in his bedroom, and Alfred came into view. "How . . . long did I sleep?" Bruce asked.

"Two days," Alfred replied. "It's your birthday."

"I only breathed the slightest amount of gas," Bruce explained. "I've felt those effects before, but this was much more potent."

"I took a blood sample and sent it to a laboratory

known for both discreet and prompt blood work," Alfred remarked, taking a sheet of paper from the night table.

Bruce took the toxicology report and skimmed it. "'Protein-based compounds' . . . It might be possible to make an antidote. I think I know how to do it."

The next day at work, he showed the report to Fox. The man's eyes widened in utter disbelief. "*This* was in your blood?"

"It's some kind of weaponized hallucinogen," Bruce replied, "administered in aerosol form. Could you synthesize an antidote?"

"This receptor's a compound I've never seen before," Fox replied. "I can do it — but it'll be hard."

Bruce nodded gratefully. "One more thing. Do you know what a Wayne Industries M-Emit 42B is?"

Fox sat at his desk and typed the name into his computer. "Hmm . . . it won't tell us. Must be a defense prototype. I'll make a couple calls to defense."

That afternoon in the DA's office, Rachel greeted Sergeant Gordon. He had phoned earlier, wanting to discuss the Falcone case.

"Counselor, thanks for seeing me," Gordon said. As Rachel closed the door, he started right in. "Will Finch go the distance on Falcone?"

"He'll have to," Rachel replied, "because of the press."

"What about Judge Faden?" Gordon asked.

"Someone gave me leverage."

"Who?"

"I'd rather not say."

Gordon shrugged. "There's a loose thread in the case. I want to see what unravels higher up. I'm told you can be trusted."

"Who told you that?" Rachel asked.

A smile creased Gordon's face. "I'd rather not say."

Rachel realized he'd seen the masked man, too. "Gordon," she said softly, "we're working for a masked vigilante. Maybe from a rival gang. What happens when he gets bolder with success and goes too far?"

"My gut says he's okay," Gordon replied, "and he's getting things moving. He took down a dozen of Gotham's most vicious wiseguys, single-handedly and without killing one of them. He's plenty bold already."

"If he takes a life," Rachel said, "it's on us."

A rap at the door stopped the conversation. It swung open, and Bruce Wayne peered in. "I'm sorry," he said. "I'll come back."

Gordon recognized the young man from the newspapers. "I was just leaving, Mr. Wayne," he insisted, rushing out of the room.

"What do you want?" Rachel snapped, closing the door behind Gordon.

"I wanted to invite you to a party," Bruce said. "Today's my birthday . . . and I wanted to apologize."

"You don't owe me an apology, Bruce. You are who you are. I don't have the right to expect anything more."

"I thought you could never quite give up on me," Bruce said.

Rachel softened. "Is the party at the house? I do miss it."

"I hate the place," Bruce replied. "I'd tear it down if I could. It's nothing without the people who made it what it was. Now there's only Alfred."

"And you," Rachel reminded him.

The door swung open, interrupting her again. "It's Falcone," Rachel's assistant announced. "They moved him to Arkham Asylum on suicide watch."

"Who authorized that?" Rachel demanded.

"Judge Bentley, on the advice of the head psychiatrist, Dr. Jonathan Crane."

This smelled of a Falcone deal — an insanity plea. "Get Crane there right now, and call Dr. Lehmann. We'll need our own assessment on the judge's desk by morning."

As her assistant scurried away, Rachel threw some papers into her briefcase and started to go. "Guess I won't make your party," she told Bruce.

She pulled the door open and hurried out, calling, "Happy birthday, Bruce," over her shoulder.

As his thirtieth birthday celebration was getting under way, Batman was perched on a landing outside Dr. Crane's office at Arkham Asylum.

Rachel was inside with Crane. Through the mike embedded in his cowl "ear," Batman could hear their two voices clearly.

"Dr. Crane," Rachel said, "about the report you filed with the judge: Is it unusual for a fifty-eight-year-old man with no history of mental illness to have a complete psychotic break?"

"In a mental asylum for the criminally insane," Crane's voice came in, "the unusual is usual."

"But isn't it convenient," Rachel pressed on, "for Falcone to suddenly develop these symptoms when he's about to be indicted?"

"Look, I doubt we're even supposed to be having this conversation," Crane said gravely, "but off the record, we're not talking about easily manufactured eccentricities. Come, I'll show you."

They were leaving to visit Falcone's cell.

Where? Batman wondered. Using his spikes, his instincts, and occasional peeks into asylum windows, he trailed the pair to a dismal holding room. Inside, Carmine Falcone lay strapped to a bed, mumbling, "Scarecrow . . . s-scarecrow . . . s-s . . ."

Rachel and Crane were already in the room. "What's 'Scarecrow'?" Rachel asked.

"He is focusing his paranoia onto an external tormentor," Crane explained, "a Jungian arche-type — a scarecrow."

"He's *drugged,*" Rachel said.

Crane nodded. "Outside, this man was a giant. In here, only the mind can grant you power. I respect the mind's power over the body. It's why I do what I do."

"What *I* do is put scum like Falcone behind bars, not in *therapy,*" Rachel shot back. "I want my own psychiatric consultant to have full access to Falcone, including blood work — tonight. I've already paged Dr. Lehmann over at County General."

"As you wish," Crane replied.

The door shut, and Batman lost audio.

Rachel emerged from the elevator with Crane into a decrepit-looking corridor. Was this a shortcut to the exit? Confused, she followed him into a vaulted room where lights hung from the rafters, illuminating rows of long tables. It must have once been a dining room for inmates, but now the tables were loaded with plastic bags, sacks of powder, scales, and aluminum barrels. Inmates, sluggish and dead-eyed, were working with the powder.

It was a drug refinery.

"This is where we make the medicine," Dr. Crane said. "Perhaps you can have some. Clear your head."

Two men appeared on either side of him, smirking and armed.

Rachel turned. She ran back through the corridor and into the elevator. She punched the button to the second floor — but nothing happened. Crane had the key.

Into the elevator doorway popped a masked face — a scarecrow mask.

As Rachel screamed, she felt a puff of gas in her face.

15

"Who knows you're here?" Crane demanded, crouched over the writhing young woman. He did not like Assistant DA Dawes — but she would soon be history. "*Who knows?*"

THHHUNNK.

The overhead lights went out, plunging the room into darkness.

Crane stood. The distant lights of Gotham slanted through the windows. "He's here," he whispered. "The Batman."

"What do we do?" asked his enforcer, whom Crane knew only as Spike.

"Call the police," Crane said flatly.

"You want the *cops* here?" asked his other enforcer, Frankie.

"Force the Batman outside," Crane said. "Let the cops wrangle him."

SSMMMMASSSHHH!

High above them, a window shattered. Spike and Frankie grabbed their guns.

Out of the darkness a small object hurtled downward. Before Spike could react, it wrapped around his ankle and yanked him upward.

CRRRACK! CRRRACK! Panicked, Frankie fired blindly.

A body hurtled downward. He jumped away, but not in time.

Spike landed on him in a bruised heap. Screaming, Frankie scrambled out from underneath — only to meet a black-gloved punch that knocked him out cold.

Standing over the two men, Batman glanced around the room. Crane and Rachel were gone. If Crane had drugged her, she wouldn't have much time.

Footsteps crept up behind him. He spun to see the scarecrow mask, the raised arm.

Batman ducked. The poison puffed harmlessly into the air as he ripped off Crane's mask, then wrenched the doctor's arm so it was pointing at his own face.

Tearing open Crane's jacket, Batman lifted up a container full of toxin, attached to a tube that ran up the jacket's sleeve. "Taste of your own medicine, Doctor?" he asked.

Crane's eyes bugged out in terror as Batman squeezed the container.

TSSSSS . . . Crane fell to the ground, gagging.

"Who are you working for?" Batman demanded.

In Crane's eyes, Batman's face was fanged, black-eyed, skeletal. "R-R-Rā's," he stammered. "Rā's . . . al Ghūl!"

Batman pulled Crane tight. "Rā's al Ghūl is dead, Crane! Who are you *really* working for?"

Crane's eyes suddenly glazed over. "Dr. Crane isn't here right now," he babbled, "but if you'd like to make an appointment —"

Crane had lost it. He was useless. Batman dropped him and turned. Rachel was running toward him, eyes ablaze, flailing her arms. She was seeing him as an enemy, a monster.

He reached out and applied a pressure grip to Rachel's neck. She fell slack. Better to keep her unconscious until he could help her.

From outside, a voice called over a bullhorn, "*BATMAN. PUT DOWN YOUR WEAPONS AND SURRENDER. YOU ARE SURROUNDED!*"

Batman scooped up Rachel and rose. Through the window, he could see dozens of cop cars, hundreds of police. He couldn't possibly escape with Rachel now, but if he didn't, she'd die.

Flass pushed through the officers to the front. His shout wafted in through the broken window. "What're you waiting for?" he demanded of the gathered cops.

"Backup," another officer replied.

"*Backup?*" Flass screamed.

"The Batman's in there," came the answer. "SWAT's on the way, but if you want to go in now . . . I'm right behind you, sir."

Flass gave him a look and shrugged, backing off.

Another officer did head inside — Gordon.

Batman knew what to do. He quietly shot a line from his grapple gun and climbed upward, carrying Rachel on his back.

Gordon moved through the dark, gun drawn, through the asylum's main building. From outside he could hear the SWAT team arrive. Before they made a mess of things, it would be better to see Batman himself.

The elevator button was dead. He'd have to take the stairs. The shooting had been on the lowest floor, the refectory.

Gordon pulled open the stairwell door and stepped onto a landing.

From behind, an arm wrapped around his chest — and suddenly he was flying upward. "Geeahhhh!" Gordon gasped.

Thump. He landed in a small storage space, high up in the rafters. He turned to face his captor —

Batman. Quickly Gordon shook off the shock. Behind him was ADA Rachel Dawes, unconscious and twitching on the floor. "What's happened to her?" he asked.

"Crane poisoned her with his toxin," Batman said. "He was the third man at the docks. I need to get her the antidote before the damage becomes permanent. She doesn't have long." He reached down and pressed a switch on his boot. A barely audible high-frequency pitch began to whine. "Get her downstairs, and meet me in the alley on the Narrows side."

"How will *you* get out?" Gordon asked.

"I called for backup," Batman replied. "Crane's been refining his toxin, stockpiling it. I don't know what he was planning, but he's working for someone else."

Gordon frowned at the obnoxious piercing squeal. "What *is* that?"

"Backup," Bruce said as he began climbing down the stairs.

Across the Gotham skies, a black cloud began to swell. It moved across the river and over the

Narrows. Answering the call, it funneled downward in a frenzy to reach the sound . . . into the windows of the Arkham refectory.

Glass showered over Batman as he descended. Below him, the SWAT burst through the stairwell door. Guns in hand, they were swallowed in a black, flapping, shrieking mass.

As the toughest of them cowered in terror, Batman calmly knelt and removed the noisemaker, tossing it over the stairway railing. The bats followed the sound downward, a solid black cloud – and Batman jumped into their midst with his cape outstretched, dropping past the SWAT team.

He landed on the floor and silently made his way out of Arkham Asylum.

16

SCCRRREEEE . . .

Batman tore out of the back alley in his Batmobile. Rachel was secured in the passenger seat, delivered safely by Gordon, but her eyes were open. Who knew what she was seeing? This could not be easy for her.

Above them, a chopper juddered loudly, bathing them with a searchlight. A cop car cut them off in front. Batman nailed the accelerator.

WHUMMMMP! His tires rolled up and over the cop car, crushing it. Smacking down on the other side, he headed for the bridge.

WEEEE-O-WEEE-O-WEEEEE-O . . .

As Batman sped into Gotham, cops closed in on all sides. "Breathe slowly," Batman said to Rachel. "Close your eyes."

"That's worse!" she shouted, gripping the dashboard in terror.

Leaning hard, he sped around a corner – and into a police roadblock.

EEEEEEEE! He steered left and powered into a parking garage, screeching up the ramps. The Batmobile was too wide. With booming explosions, it took out cement pillars like toothpicks, until it sprang onto the roof.

"What're you doing?" Rachel screamed.

"Shortcut," Batman replied. "Trust me."

From the garage exit, cop cars emerged and formed a blockade. Batman checked his GPS. He swung forward and sat in the glass bubble of the front driving pod. There, he threw the jet engine switch.

SSSSHHHHOOOOM!

Flaps flared out of the car's front and rear. The

wheels shot off the ground — and the Batmobile was airborne!

"Aaaaghhh!" Rachel screamed.

They landed with a thud on the next roof and quickly launched into the air again over another gap. Batman peered ahead, over the cityscape. The freeway was close, next to a tall building with a slanted tile roof.

SSSSHHHHOOOOM!

The Batmobile smacked down on the tiled roof, its wheels spinning, its right side angled downward as it rode across the tiles. With another thrust of the rockets, they launched onto the elevated freeway, thumping down into the center lane.

Cars skidded and steered away as Batman floored the accelerator.

CHUCKA-CHUCKA-CHUCKA-CHUCKA . . .

Directly overhead, the helicopter bore down on them.

The traffic was heavy — too heavy. In the rear-view mirror, Batman saw cop cars gaining. He slipped back into the regular driver's seat and glanced at Rachel. Her eyes were blank, her breathing shallow. "Stay with me," he murmured.

Slowing the Batmobile, he cut the lights. The car would be totally black now, an absence of light. Cop cars pulled up on either side. Inside, the officers were angry, baffled, *not seeing him.*

Then, from above, the chopper light bathed the Batmobile.

"There he is!" a cop's voice shouted.

Batman lunged into the pod seat. He tapped the jet button just enough to send a jet spray into his pursuers' windshields and propel the Batmobile through a hole in the traffic.

Swerving down the next exit ramp, the Batmobile screeched onto the road and plunged into a wooded area.

Batman cut the lights again. In the night-vision monitor, the surroundings were spectral, flickering green shapes.

"Just hold on!" he told Rachel.

He yanked a lever, releasing a ground anchor that dug into the road. The Batmobile whipped around to the right, zooming down a dirt path. Trees hung over the road — in the monitor they waved like pea-colored ghosts.

Rachel was sobbing now. She was losing it.

Batman's eyes darted ahead, to a lookout over a river gorge. He jammed the accelerator, speeding faster . . . faster. . . .

Rachel twisted in her seat, cowering.

The Batmobile shot over the ledge, its wheels spinning, arcing high through the air, over the river — and plunged straight into the face of a waterfall!

The water's powerful crash nearly drowned out Rachel's scream. Shuddering, feeling as if it would explode in a shower of metal, the Batmobile thumped onto a solid floor.

A dry, solid floor — inside the Batcave. Hooking a steel cable, the ground anchors yanked the car to a halt.

Rachel was out cold.

The canopy of the Batmobile hissed open in three sections, like insect wings. Batman lifted Rachel from the cockpit. Stepping down onto the shale, he carried her into the cavern and laid her down on the worktable. Hoping it wasn't too late, he reached for the antidote.

17

Arkham swirled with cops. The bats were gone, and so was most of the SWAT team. Gordon, still reeling from the sight of Batman's vehicle, checked in with the detective in charge of Crane. "Is he cooperating?" Gordon asked.

The detective gestured to the corner of a cell block, where Crane chattered nonsense. "If by *cooperating*, you mean chewing his way through three sets of restraints, then yes, he's cooperating."

A young cop rushed over to Gordon. "Sir!" he shouted. "There's something you should take a look at!"

The cop led Gordon into another enormous room, its floor pitted with rectangular holes trimmed in chipped blue-and-white marble. An abandoned bathhouse, from the looks of it.

In the center was a large pool. At the bottom lay several aluminum barrels, surrounding a massive hole.

Gordon climbed down and peered into the hole. Below, through layers of dug-out earth, a powerful stream flowed toward Gotham. "Looks like they tapped the mains," he muttered. But for what? Transportation? Germ warfare?

Gordon sat up, eyeing the aluminum barrels.

"*Get me somebody at the water board!*" he bellowed.

***

Rachel's eyelids fluttered open. Shapes began to form, blurry and dark — a writhing black mass attached to a cragged ceiling.

Bats.

She groaned. Her head felt as if it had been split with an ax.

"How do you feel?" asked a familiar voice.

Forcing her eyes open, she looked into the mask of Batman. He had her in this cave . . . *on a table.*

"Where are we?" she asked. "Why did you bring me here?"

"If I hadn't, your mind would be lost," Batman replied. "You were poisoned."

"I remember . . . nightmares. This mask . . . it was *Crane*! I have to tell the police —" She swung her legs around but stumbled trying to get up.

Batman caught her in his arms and set her gently back on the table. "Rest. Gordon has Crane."

She tried to look into his face, to see his eyes. But he was backing away into the shadows. "Is Sergeant Gordon your friend?" she asked.

"I don't have the luxury of friends," the strange man answered.

"Why did you save my life?" Rachel pressed on, watching his silhouette.

"Gotham needs you," he replied.

"And you serve Gotham?"

"I serve justice."

Hearing that kind of statement usually set her off. To her, vigilantes were criminals — but this guy was different. "Perhaps you do," she said softly.

"I'm going to give you a sedative to put you back to sleep," Batman said, holding up the two vials. "You'll wake up back at home, and when you do, get these to Gordon. Trust no one else."

"What are they?" Rachel asked.

"The antidote. One for Gordon to inoculate himself, the other to start mass production." For a second, as Batman handed her the vials, she could see his eyes. There was something familiar about them. "Crane was just a pawn," he said. "He was working for someone else."

"Something al Ghūl . . ." Rachel murmured, remembering what she'd heard.

Batman cocked his head curiously. "Rā's al Ghūl. It's not him. He's dead. I watched him die."

As Batman stepped closer with her sedative,

Rachel closed her eyes. She trusted him, and she could use the sleep.

Inside the old asylum bathhouse, Sergeant Gordon barked into the phone at the water board officials. "Someone's been dumping a dangerous contaminant into the supply from this location for days, maybe weeks," he explained.

"If that's true," one of the techs replied, "then it's already spread through the whole system. But no one's reported any effects."

Gordon thought hard. Poisons, he knew, came in many shapes and forms. "It must be like chlorine or fluoride," he said. "Harmless to drink but deadly to breathe. Wake up your boss, see if there's a way to flush out the system!"

Hanging up the phone, Gordon noticed something odd in the room — a large shipping crate near the wall. "Open that up," he commanded a nearby cop, who immediately gathered partners to dismantle the crate.

Inside was a giant machine, about the size of a van, with a Wayne Industries decal on the side. "What on earth is it?" the cop asked.

"I don't know," Gordon said, "but nobody gets near it, understand? We're closing the bridges, locking down the whole island!"

Bruce took the dumbwaiter up from the Batcave and emerged into his study through a secret revolving bookcase. In the enclosed veranda outside, his birthday party was in full swing. He would put in an appearance and then split. He had a long night ahead of him.

Alfred offered a white shirt and dinner jacket, which Bruce hurriedly put on. "Rachel's sedated," Bruce said. "You can take her home. Tell your staff to stop serving drinks after the cake. Is Fox still here?"

Alfred nodded toward the crowd, where Fox hovered at the buffet. Bruce stepped out onto the veranda. "There he is!" a guest shouted.

Instantly voices began singing "Happy Birthday," accompanied by an orchestra. Shaking hands and grinning, Bruce moved through the crowd toward Fox. "Any word on that . . . item?" he said under his breath.

Fox leaned closer. "My contact in heavy weapons says it's a microwave emitter. It vaporizes water."

Bruce's mind raced. Vaporizing water was harmless — but other substances, when changed from liquid to gas, could be lethal. And if any of those substances were *in* the water . . .

"Could you use the emitter to put a biological agent into the air?" Bruce asked.

"Sure, if the water supply were poisoned before you vaporized it," Fox said.

Poison. *A whole city?*

From behind him, Mr. Earle called out in a jolly voice, "Happy birthday, Bruce — not everybody thought you'd make it this far!"

"Sorry to disappoint," Bruce said, turning to greet him. "How did the stock offering go?"

"The price soared. A variety of funds and bro-kerages bought. It's all a bit technical — but the key thing is, our company's future is secure!"

As Earle turned and shook hands with Fox, Bruce slipped away. He did not hear what Earle actually said: "Fox, forget about kissing up to Wayne. I've put you on top of the early retirement list."

Across town, Rachel awoke in her own bed to the sound of a car engine. Groggily she peered out the window and saw Bruce's Rolls Royce leaving, with Alfred at the wheel.

On her bedside table, two vials came into focus.

Antidote. For Gordon.

Suddenly, Rachel was wide awake. She didn't have much time. Hopping out of bed, she stumbled to the door.

As Bruce strode toward the library, a woman grabbed his arm — Mrs. Delane, an old friend of

Father's. "Bruce!" her fluty voice piped. "There's somebody here you simply *must* meet!"

"I can't just now –" Bruce protested, but he immediately swallowed his words. With her was a man whose jacket sported a blue poppy.

"Now, am I pronouncing it right?" Mrs. Delane trilled. "Mister . . . al Ghūl?"

"You're not Rā's al Ghūl," Bruce said, looking into the face of a man who bore a striking resemblance to his erstwhile foe. "He's dead."

Mrs. Delane's smile faded.

Another voice called from Bruce's right. "But is Rā's al Ghūl immortal? Are his methods supernatural?"

Bruce spun around and came face-to-face with someone he did know. Ducard.

18

"Immortal?" Bruce repeated, moving closer to the supremely calm Ducard. "Or are his methods cheap parlor tricks — to conceal your true identity, *Rā's?*"

"Ducard" was a false identity. He was Rā's al Ghūl — and as he took Bruce by the arm, they left behind a stunned and speechless Mrs. Delane. "Surely you don't begrudge me dual identities?" Rā's al Ghūl asked. "I've been admiring your work, even as it's interfered with my plans. You were my greatest student . . . until you betrayed me."

Now Bruce became aware of people who didn't

belong here — faces from another time, another life. Ninjas. Members of the League of Shadows.

The guests were in danger. They had to go. Fast.

Thinking fast, Bruce clinked a glass and began a loud toast — which quickly became a string of insults. He called them leeches, hangers-on, people who wanted to use their connection to the Wayne name for their own profit and glory.

It didn't take long to clear the house. In minutes, their cars were driving away.

"They don't have long to live," Rā's al Ghūl said with amusement, watching them leave. "Your antics at the asylum have forced my hand."

Bruce began piecing together the puzzle. "Crane was working for *you*!"

Rā's al Ghūl nodded, strolling toward the library. "His toxin is derived from the organic compound in our blue poppies. Crane was able to weaponize the compound — but he just wanted money and power. I told him the plan was to hold the city for ransom, but in fact —"

"You're going to unleash Crane's poison on the entire city — and destroy millions of lives!"

"No. Billions of lives. Gotham will tear itself apart through fear — but that will just be the beginning. The world will watch in terror as the greatest city falls. Anarchy and chaos will spread. Mankind will ravage itself, the species will be culled . . . and the balance of nature restored. The planet will be saved for all species."

Bruce couldn't believe what he was hearing. "You're inhuman!"

"Don't question my humanity, Bruce," Rā's al Ghūl said levelly. "I saved you from that fetid hole I found you in. I showed you a path and took away your fear. *I made you what you are.* And in return, you attacked me and burned my home. Since then, you've used my skills and techniques to interfere with my plans, plans in which you were supposed to play a part."

He nodded to his men. Obediently, they began setting fire to the drapes.

"What part was that, Rā's?" Bruce spat. "To put

my company at your disposal? To obtain your microwave emitter and plant it somewhere in Gotham?"

Rā's al Ghūl sighed. "You were supposed to be Gotham's destroyer. Instead you became her only protector."

"You underestimate Gotham!"

"Gotham is helpless without you. That's why I'm here. We've infiltrated every aspect of the city's infrastructure. *You* underestimate Gotham's corruption. . . ."

Miles away, four armed SWAT members stood guarding the emitter. One of them checked his watch and nodded to a partner, who quickly powered up the machine.

A protesting SWAT member — the only one — was taken care of by a close-range bullet. Moving with ninja precision, the men began placing explosive charges along the wall.

At the same time, high above the city, a train driver checked *his* watch. "This train is no longer in service," he announced.

To a chorus of disappointed groans, he opened the doors and waited for the passengers to leave. The train would be needed by Rā's al Ghūl.

Slowly, service by service, the city ground to a halt.

19

Gordon huddled against the side of the building. The machine was secure. The water board had been notified. The Narrows was sealed off. Crane was neutralized.

Still, they hadn't found Crane's boss, the mastermind behind this whole scheme. *Who was it?*

Out of the rainy darkness, Rachel Dawes ran toward him. She looked normal again. "How are you?" Gordon asked.

"Better, thanks to Batman," she said, pulling the two vials from her pocket. "He sent me with doses of the antidote for you —"

Before she could finish, the ground shook with a deafening *BOOM!*

Gordon bolted toward the bathhouse.

"Gordon, wait!" Rachel shouted from behind him.

Smoke billowed from a hole in the building's back wall. A squadron of cops, including Gordon, marched toward it.

Three SWAT members were pushing the machine through the hole.

Impostors.

Gordon drew his gun and fired. The bullets ricocheted off the wall as the men dived behind the machine.

The cops moved closer, but they held fire for fear of hitting the machine. As they scattered around the room, one of the SWAT members yanked a switch on a control panel.

The machine whirred. A pulse shot out – not light or water, but something that seemed to vibrate the air itself.

FOOOOM!

Gordon hit the ground. Just outside the building, a manhole cover exploded on a geyser of steam.

FOOOOM!

A fire hydrant exploded into shards.

FOOOOM! FOOOOM! FOOOOM!

All around the asylum, cops ducked for shelter as steam gushed upward, enveloping the Narrows in a mushroom cloud.

A smaller, more acrid cloud hissed from the refectory, where the drugs had been stored.

Gordon caught a sharp whiff, and he began coughing.

BEEEP . . . BEEEP . . . BEEEP . . .

In the control room of the Gotham Water Board, an alarm went off. The tech officers leaned over the master map. A bright dot glowed in the area of the Narrows. It looked like some kind of pressure under the island. As if the water were boiling.

The valves into the city were holding, though. For now.

On the Wayne estate, flames shot up the stone walls of the stately manor, igniting the roof tiles, exploding the windows. The veranda was now in flames. Smoke crept in through the library window.

Bruce knew this was payback for what he'd done to the monastery. "So you've come to kill me?" he demanded.

Rā's al Ghūl's eyes flickered with a heavy sadness. "To bring you back to us, Bruce. To help us save the planet before man destroys it with his greed, his pollution, his weaponry." Rā's al Ghūl took a sword from one of the ninjas. Pressing the point to his own throat, he offered the handle to Bruce. "You still doubt me? Apply a few pounds of pressure. Buy your precious city a reprieve. Kill me. Then you'll understand how simple it is to do what's necessary."

Bruce held the sword firmly. Rage coursed through him. One thrust would end it. Rā's al Ghūl deserved it.

No.

He slackened his grip. He couldn't. That would be *his* way of doing things. "I will not take life," Bruce said. "I will not be a part of this."

"But you already are," Rā's al Ghūl said. "You've given Gotham a potent symbol of fear."

"I frighten criminals —"

"You frighten *everybody*! A giant, vengeful bat? What better apocalyptic symbol to haunt Gotham's dreams as panic takes hold?"

Defiantly, Bruce lowered the sword. Rā's al Ghūl's expression instantly hardened. He pulled on the handle of his cane — unsheathing another sword. "Then *die* with Gotham."

Rā's al Ghūl struck downward, knocking the sword from Bruce's hand. Bruce jumped away, scooping up the weapon.

CLANK!

Rā's al Ghūl's thrust connected with Bruce's blade, spitting blue sparks. He lunged toward Bruce, slashing and spinning.

Flames crept across the ceiling's oaken beams. The heat was building. Soon the room — the house — would blow.

Bruce pressed Rā's al Ghūl to the wall of the library, then backed away as his nemesis lunged forward. Off balance, Rā's al Ghūl fell to the floor. Bruce stood over him, holding the sword to his throat. "Perhaps you taught me too well," he said.

"Or perhaps you'll never learn," Rā's al Ghūl said with a calm smile, "to mind your surroundings as well as your opponent."

CRRRRAAACK!

A section of the burning roof collapsed. Bruce looked up, but not in time.

The last thing he saw before going unconscious was the pained look on Rā's al Ghūl's face.

"Rest easy, friend," he said, then hurried out of the smoky building. "No one comes out — make sure!" he shouted to his men, racing to a helicopter that had just made a landing.

"They created a smokescreen in the Narrows,"

the pilot reported, "and they're moving the emitter into place for your run."

Rā's al Ghūl stepped into the passenger seat. As the chopper lifted off the ground, he watched Wayne Manor burn.

THUMP.

The golf club connected squarely with the back of the young ninja's head.

"I sincerely hope you're not from the fire department," Alfred said to the inert young man, who until now had been guarding the entrance to Wayne Manor — or what was left of it.

Dropping the club, Alfred ran to the library, where he'd last seen Master Wayne. He spotted the Gucci-shoed legs protruding from under a pile of burning debris.

Alfred knelt, curling his fingers under the mass. But it was far too heavy.

"*Master Wayne!*" He slapped the young heir's face until his eyes finally flickered. "Sir, whatever is the point of all those push-ups if you can't even —"

With a grunt, Bruce pushed upward. The beam jerked — and then crashed beside him onto the floor.

The Persian rug was in flames now, and the cherry-wood parquet floor beneath. Alfred tried not to think of the waste, the enormous loss. . . .

Bruce pressed four keys on the piano — the combination that made the bookcase swing open. The two men ducked inside and onto the elevator, then dropped downward into the coolness of the Batcave.

As they landed, Bruce's eyes winced at the sound of crashing timbers above. The library, it would seem, was now rubble. "What have I done, Alfred?" he whispered. "Everything my father and his father built . . ."

Alfred struggled to stand. His legs ached, but his heart ached more. "The Wayne legacy," he said, "is more than bricks and mortar, sir."

"I thought I could help Gotham," Bruce said. "But I've failed."

With an effort he didn't know he had, a strength that reached back through generations of his own family, Alfred looked resolutely into the young man's face. "And . . . why do we fall, sir? *So that we might better learn to pick ourselves up.*"

Bruce's eyes were bloodshot. "Still haven't given up on me?"

"Never."

Alfred's hand trembled as he extended it to help the young man up.

Outside the asylum, Rachel had to wave away the fog just to see. Someone had let the inmates loose. Through Arkham's windows, she saw them rioting, screaming, dancing.

A police horse came cantering toward her on the cracked asphalt. Dr. Crane was in the saddle, cackling, the burlap mask firmly on his face. "Crane!" she cried out.

He hissed. "*Ssssscarecrow.*"

Lifting her taser stun gun, she shot. Crane jerked with the impact and fell to the ground. The startled horse took off at a gallop – dragging Crane on the ground by his stirrups into the fog.

Above her, a monorail train stopped. A team of masked men under the lead car began attaching a huge machine onto a hoist, which would lift it to the train. *They're looting,* Rachel thought, *despite all these cops around.* Only in Gotham.

Frantically looking for Gordon, she raced around the building – and she found him, coughing and choking, near a gaping hole in the wall. He turned to her, his eyes wide with fright.

She knew from his expression that he'd breathed the poison. "Gordon, it's me – Rachel! I have the antidote!"

He tried to run. She struggled to keep him still, but he was at least fifty pounds heavier. "Stay calm," she said. "I can help you."

FFFWWOOOOSH!

The Batmobile rocketed through the waterfall, sending out a violent spray as it soared to the opposite road. Pedal to the floor, Batman raced for the Narrows. Even from here he could see the steam cloud above the island.

He could not see the chopper cutting through that cloud. In the passenger seat, Rā's al Ghūl put on a gas mask in preparation for the final plan.

Sitting against the broken wall of Arkham Asylum, Rachel slapped Gordon's face. He was groggy, sluggish.

The screaming inmates were coming closer on both sides — *stalking,* preparing to attack. Their eyes were bloodshot, their faces pale. They had been inside, exposed to the poison like Gordon.

Rachel slapped Gordon harder, screaming his name. His head lolled to one side, and his eyes opened. "Rachel?"

"YEEAHHHHHH!"

The inmates attacked in a running charge. Rachel screamed.

WHOMMMM!

From out of the cloud hurtled the Batmobile. It skidded to a stop inches from Rachel.

The inmates dove away as the door flew open and Batman jumped out. A brick clipped him on the side of his mask. Shrieking, frightened, the inmates attacked him with whatever projectiles they could find.

Batman lifted Rachel off the ground. He fired his grappling gun upward and they soared into the air — and onto one of the towering spires of Arkham Asylum.

Below them, Gordon shook off his delirium. As his vision cleared, he saw the hulking emitter being loaded onto the monorail train, which was pointed toward the city.

Pushing himself off the ground, Gordon stumbled toward his car.

On the Arkham rooftop, Rachel was hyperventilating. The place was high, *way* high, jutting above the vapor cloud. In the distance she could see Wayne Tower and the spoke-wheel train system that circled the metropolis — all of it cloudless against the night sky.

The vapor had not yet reached Gotham.

"They're going to unleash the toxin on the entire city," Batman said. "I have to find the microwave emitter."

"They were lifting a machine up to the tracks!" Rachel blurted.

A metallic noise screeched from below as the monorail began to inch forward.

Batman tensed, his eyes following the track's path into the heart of Gotham. "Of course — the monorail. The track runs directly over the water mains! He's going to drive that thing straight into Wayne Tower and blow the main hub, creating enough toxin to blanket the entire city!"

CHHHOOM! CHHHOOM! CHHHOOM!

Under the train, manhole covers exploded upward like flipped coins as the emitter vaporized the water beneath.

Batman stepped to the roof's edge. The train was several stories below, pulling farther away.

"Wait!" Rachel cried. As he turned, she reached up to his face. "You could die. At least tell me your name."

"It's not who I am underneath," he said, "but what I *do* that defines me."

Her words.

"Bruce," she said — but he was gone, falling into the mist.

In the vapor-saturated air, his visibility was nil. He slid his gloves into the activating pockets of his cape.

The fabric went rigid, jerking him upward like a parachute. He held out his arms, controlling the wing structure, catching the wind, sailing into the clear air over the Gotham River.

The monorail was below him, its lights snaking along the track, crossing the shoreline into the city streets. He angled toward it, gliding fast.

FOOOSH! FOOOSH!

Geysers sprang up around him, causing him to

bank left and right. As the train passed through buildings, he veered around them.

Wayne Tower loomed closer. By now the pressure on the hub would be enormous. He leaned into the wind, until he was over the train's last car. Quickly, he de-electrified the memory fabric and fell.

Landing on the roof, he held tight. The wind pressed against his face as the train passed through a building tunnel.

CRACK! CRACK! CRACK!

Bullets blasted through the roof from inside. He felt three of them hit his chest.

Groaning, he fell from the train.

In the rear car of the speeding monorail, three warriors from the League of Shadows gazed through the bullet holes in the roof. They saw nothing but the stars. Whatever had been up there was gone.

CLANK.

They jumped. A thick metal hook had pierced the floor.

Racing to the window, they glanced out to see the man they knew as Batman hanging from a long cable, over crowds of gawkers. He flew outward as the track curved, dodging streetlights and awnings, as manhole covers and fire hydrants burst upward in the train's wake.

A truck kept pace with the train a half block ahead. Out of the back window emerged a ninja soldier with a rocket-propelled grenade launcher. Raising the sight to his eyes, he took careful aim.

A block away, Gordon tore around a corner in his car. He had broken every traffic law in the book to get there. A truck sped into the intersection, directly in his path.

He stepped on the accelerator.

BLAM!

The impact of Gordon's sedan knocked the truck off the road. From its back window shot a grenade — way off target — as the truck crashed and exploded in a fireball.

Shaken but alive, Gordon watched Batman soar safely above the truck's flames.

Fighting against the force of the train's pull, Batman tried to haul the grappling gun to his belt where he could attach it to a retractor. Just ahead loomed the brick wall of another tunnel. If he stayed hanging there, it would flatten him.

The front car disappeared into the tunnel's blackness . . . the second car . . . third. . . .

CLICK.

The gun connected, just as the last car entered the tunnel. Batman shot upward, feeling the whoosh of the passing tunnel wall as he clutched the side of the train.

He leaped into the last car, making quick work of an unsuspecting ninja team. Then he worked his way forward, car by car.

He paused in the opening just before the first car. Inside, Rā's al Ghūl turned. The smug expression vanished from his face. "You," he said.

Without answering, Batman leaped out of sight, onto the roof.

Rā's al Ghūl scrambled outside and upward, joining him. His black-cowled former pupil stood like a specter, cloak flapping in the night. Rā's al Ghūl drew his sword. "You took my advice about theatricality a bit literally, don't you think?"

Batman lunged. With the sword in one hand and

the cane in the other, Rā's al Ghūl held him off and swung.

As they sped through a tunnel, buffeted by wind, Batman caught the cane in the hooks of his gauntlet. He lifted his arm upward and the cane went flying.

"Familiar," Rā's al Ghūl said mockingly.

He thrust, and Batman jumped to the front edge of the train. His foot slipped on the slick surface and he lost his balance.

Rā's al Ghūl took advantage. He brought the sword down over his nemesis's head — hard.

Batman crossed both his arms in front.

CHANK. The sword stuck fast in the hooks of both his gauntlets.

"Don't you have anything new?" Rā's al Ghūl taunted.

"How about *this*?" Batman said, yanking his arms in opposite directions.

Rā's al Ghūl sword split in two — and he stumbled back with the force of the jolt.

Batman spun around. Wayne Tower was four blocks

away. He dropped to his chest, leaning over the front of the train. Aiming carefully, he shot his grappling-gun cable into the car's guide wheels.

The hook made contact with a loud metallic *SHHHUNK*. Sparking, screeching, the wheels pulled out the line of cable. The train juddered on the track, slowing but not stopping. It wasn't going to be enough. The cable wouldn't hold.

"*What are you doing?*" Rā's al Ghūl shouted desperately from behind him.

"What's necessary," Batman replied.

He threw the entire grappling-gun apparatus into the path of the guide wheel. The train lurched, hopping off its rail, smashing against the concrete guides.

Rā's al Ghūl dove onto Batman, pinning him against the roof. Batman rolled upright, but Rā's al Ghūl's grip was deadly tight. His thumbs dug into the flesh above Batman's neckpiece, and he gagged, losing breath, losing sight. . . .

"*Are you afraid?*" Rā's al Ghūl hissed.

"Yes," Batman rasped, his strength ebbing. He loosened his own grip and slipped his hand down his cloak to the activating pockets. "But not of you."

The cloak went rigid. It caught the wind of the still-moving train, and Batman was yanked upward, into the air.

Rā's al Ghūl looked up in surprise, anger . . . and terror.

With a sickening noise, the train broke through the guide rail. It plunged to the street, hurtling toward the open marble expanse of Wayne Plaza.

CRAAAAASSSHH!

The impact shook the ground as the train exploded into flames.

Rising upward on the warming air, Batman could hear the lingering death scream of Rā's al Ghūl echo through the canyons of Gotham.

23

The ailing city slowly began to heal. Falcone was off the streets. The path to destruction had been thwarted. Gotham seemed like a place worth saving, and people were rolling up their sleeves to help.

The pulverized train had been cleared, the charred remains of Rā's al Ghūl and his men taken to a morgue. Construction on the destroyed Wayne Plaza was already in its beginning stages.

Lucius Fox was proud to be in charge. On ground-breaking day, as he surveyed the scene, he spotted Mr. Earle huffing toward him, wearing his usual gray suit.

"This is a hard-hat area," Fox reminded him.

"What are *you* doing here, Fox?" Earle retorted. "I seem to remember firing you."

"Might be something to do with my new job as head of Wayne Industries," Fox replied. "Didn't you get the memo?"

Earle glared at him. "Whose authority?"

Fox pointed at a Rolls Royce idling nearby. Bruce Wayne was in the backseat, stifling a grin.

"You think you have authority to decide who runs this company, Bruce?" Earle demanded.

"It *is* my company," Bruce replied.

"Not anymore. Wayne Industries went public a week ago —"

"I bought most of the shares," said Bruce. "A controlling interest, in fact — through various charitable foundations, trusts, and so forth. Look, it's all a bit technical, but the important thing is, my company's future is secure."

In the front seat, a smiling Alfred started up the car and drove away, leaving Earle speechless.

That afternoon, Bruce placed a board over the old well at Wayne Manor. His home was a smoking ruin, a skeleton of twisted steel among piles of stone. Inside, Alfred supervised salvage workers.

Bruce heard footsteps and glanced up to see Rachel approaching. He hadn't heard her drive up, but he was happy to see her. "Do you remember the day I fell?" he asked.

"Of course," Rachel replied.

"As I lay there, I *knew* . . . I could sense that things would never be the same."

Rachel cocked her head curiously. "What did you find down there?"

Bruce placed another board across the well, closing the gap completely. "Childhood's end."

Rachel took his arm, and they walked toward the house. "The day you left Gotham," she said, "the day Chill was murdered, I said terrible things."

"True things," Bruce said. "You made me see that justice is about more than my own pain and anger."

"Well, you proved me wrong," she said softly. "Your father *would* be proud of you. Just as I am."

Bruce stopped. He turned toward her, looking into eyes that were deeper than oceans and sweeter than the night. He decided to do what he had wanted to do for years. He kissed her. He felt as if everything he had ever endured had been for this moment.

When they finally separated, Rachel turned away. "Between Batman and Bruce Wayne," she said, "there's no room for me."

"Rachel, I chose this life. I can give it up."

She touched his face gently. "You didn't choose the life, Bruce. It was thrust upon you, the way greatness often is. You've given this city hope, and now she's depending on you. We all are. Good-bye, Bruce."

Walking away, Rachel looked toward the house. "What will you do?"

"I'm going to rebuild it," Bruce replied, "just the way it was. Brick for brick."

Rachel smiled. He watched her go, taking his heart with her. A moment later, Alfred walked up beside him. "Just the way it was, sir?" he asked.

"Yes . . . why?" Bruce asked.

"I thought we might take the opportunity of making some improvements . . . to the foundation."

Bruce smiled. "Could you mean the southeast corner?"

"Precisely, sir," Alfred said.

Epilogue

That night, Batman received a signal from Gordon — a bat shape projected on a passing cloud. He was on the roof of the station house in minutes, where Gordon was manning a police spotlight partially covered by a black bat-shaped stencil.

"Nice," Batman remarked.

"Couldn't find any mob bosses to strap to the light," Gordon said.

"What can I do for you, Sergeant?"

Gordon flicked off the light. "It's *Lieutenant* now. Commissioner Loeb had to promote me. He also had to disband the task force hunting you. Amazing what saving a city can do for your image."

"Then things are better?"

"You've started something," Gordon said. "Bent cops are running scared, there's hope on the streets. . . ." His words hung uncertainly in the air.

"But?" Batman asked.

"But there's a lot of weirdness out there right now. We still haven't picked up Crane or half the inmates of Arkham that he freed —"

"We will. Gotham will return to normal."

"Will it? What about escalation? We start carrying semiautomatics, they buy automatics. We start wearing Kevlar, they buy armor-piercing rounds. . . ."

"And?" Batman prodded.

"And . . . you're wearing a mask and jumping off rooftops." Gordon pulled a clear plastic evidence bag from his pocket. "Take this guy. Armed robbery, double homicide. He's got a taste for theatrics, like you. Leaves a calling card."

He handed Batman the bag. Inside was a playing card.

A joker.

"I'll look into it," Bruce said.

As he pocketed the card and stepped up to the balustrade, Gordon called out, "You know, I never said thank you."

Batman gazed out over Gotham. His cloak snapped in the breeze. "And you'll never have to."

As Batman dropped from the rooftop, gliding on the night wind, Lieutenant Gordon smiled.

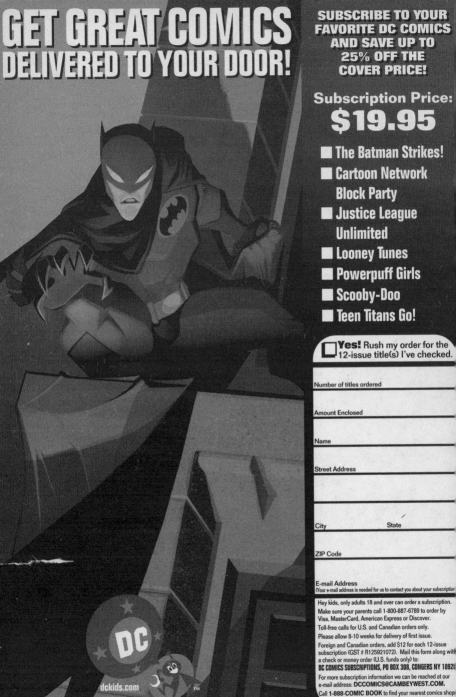